A Tortoise for the
Queen of Tonga

A Tortoise for the Queen of Tonga

JULIA WHITTY

A Mariner Original
HOUGHTON MIFFLIN COMPANY
Boston · New York
2002

Visit our Web site: www.houghtonmifflinbooks.com.

Whitty, Julia.
A tortoise for the Queen of Tonga / Julia Whitty.
p. cm.
"A Mariner original."
ISBN 0-618-11980-9
1. Animals — Fiction. 2. Human-animal relationships — Fiction.
3. Nature — Effect of human beings on — Fiction. I. Title.
PS3623.H588   T67 2002
813'.6—dc21   2001051607

Book design by Melissa Lotfy
Typefaces: Minion, Eva Antiqua

Printed in the United States of America

QUM 10 9 8 7 6 5 4 3 2 1

For my parents, Mark and Patience,
with love and gratitude

ACKNOWLEDGMENTS

Special thanks to fellow scribes Jill Koenigsdorf, Lillian Ho Wan, and Karen Laws Callaway, for their heartfelt critique. To Hardy Jones for giving me the room to open this door. To Mary Catherine Siebel, Richard Upton, and Karen Jones for reading and encouragement. To Katherine Kidde for all her efforts and support. To Heidi Pitlor for her elegant editorial suggestions. And to Liz Duvall for her subtle finishing touches.

CONTENTS

A Tortoise for the Queen of Tonga

SHE DIED in the palace gardens in 1966, of extreme old age and a heart that had swelled insupportably from nearly two centuries of loneliness. For a day no one noticed, not because she was neglected but because her metabolism was so inert that immobility did not arouse suspicion. The crabs discovered her first, hordes of frenetic, land-dwelling red crabs with pincers for cutlery. The dogs found her next, but because they neither bayed nor howled, they kept the secret to themselves. Only when the pigs got wind of it and began to squeal with excitement did the queen's gardener rouse himself from the shade of a casuarina tree and stroll with detached curiosity toward the community of living things that had gathered to feast on the remains of the tortoise.

"Tu'i Malila is dead," the gardener announced to the queen's secretary.

"Your Royal Highness," said the queen's secretary to the king, "Tu'i Malila is dead."

"Royal Wife and Queen," said the king to the queen, "Tu'i Malila is dead."

The queen did not rise from her wrought iron chaise under the banyan tree, but she did signal to her ladies in waiting to stop swirling the palm-frond fans around her head as her huge moonface quivered and her dark eyes filled with tears.

For more than two decades, long after the pigs had been spit-roasted and the *umu* ovens had been dug for the funeral feast, which drew nobility from all over Tongatapu, the giant tortoise lay where she had died. In the course of time her empty carapace became as much a feature of the palace gardens as the huge Norfolk Island pines and the red gingerbread gables of the wooden palace. Generations of princes and princesses played hide-and-seek behind her shell, until in 1988 she was moved to the new Tonga National Center outside Nuku'alofa, where her remains were displayed alongside portraits of the monarchs. Visitors wondered at the vast parchment of her shell, its surface scarred, chipped, burned, and in places worn as thin as a fingernail from her encounters with pirates, explorers, missionaries, kings, queens, and hurricanes.

Captain James Cook bought the giant tortoise in 1776 from a Dutch merchant in Cape Town, South Africa, as he embarked on his third and final voyage of the Pacific. She was not yet an adult, although she was probably thirty years old, her skin young and supple with the soft patina of sea glass. The Dutch merchant had bought her from English pirates, who had manhandled her from her home on the atoll of Aldabra, off the coast of Africa. She spent weeks in the dark bellies of various ships, trussed, unwatered, and unfed, panicking at the strange motion of the sea, the perpetual blackness, the stench of men, the attacks of sea lice and rats. The sailors did not treat her as a living thing. They kicked her, or carelessly dripped hot lamp oil on her, and laughed.

She retreated into a hallucinogenic state in which she could see in her mind's eye the yellow light of Aldabra, the turquoise sea, the opalescent sky decorated with the black kites of soaring frigate birds. In that quiet world the rumble of surf on the barrier reef was punctuated only by the trilling calls of terns or the scratching of crabs scrambling across the rocks or the soft thud of giant tortoises settling down for a nap. Most afternoons brought showers and thunder, but even those were soothing sounds marking the passage of day toward night. Nothing she had known in her native home could have prepared her for the din of a wooden ship in rough seas, crowded with men and livestock.

Captain Cook took her aboard along with a menagerie of sheep, goats, cattle, horses, and chickens, which turned his ship, *Resolution,* into a floating ark. The giant tortoise was considered a particularly valuable part of his oceangoing savings account, because she could survive up to a year in the hold without food or water. When called upon in a time of need, she would become turtle soup.

The sailors lowered her into the dank hold and the hatches dropped down onto darkness. *Resolution* plunged south into the mountainous waves of the Roaring Forties, where the ship began to leak, squalls tore the mizzen topmast off, the horses tap-danced nervously, and the sheep shivered and died. When a fog as dense as smoke settled over the sea, *Resolution* and her companion ship, *Discovery,* maintained contact with each other by the steady firing of their guns.

Months later the ships reached the tropical islands of Tonga, where William Bligh, the young master of *Resolution,* oversaw the tricky business of getting the tortoise onto a launch. Two sailors ran the deck winch while three others waited below in the open boat. The tortoise emerged from the darkness with her head drawn deep into her shell and her eyes squeezed shut.

"A dozen lashes to any fool who drops it," shouted Bligh as the sailors heaved. But the ropes shifted, the knots slipped, and the tortoise crashed onto the boat's thwart, chipping a bony plate on the left side of her carapace.

Captain Cook accepted a gift a day from the Tu'i Tonga, the king of the islands of Tonga, which Cook called "the Friendly Isles." He accepted a sacred red feather bonnet, bowls of intoxicating kava to drink, and exquisite paintings on bark, called *tapa*. In return, the king took few gifts, showing no interest in the novelties that his people borrowed with infuriating regularity from *Resolution:* cats, muskets, buttons, nails, anchors. The king did not care for such things. He accepted only one small glass bowl, some livestock, and the tortoise, which Cook calculated that he would no longer need now that the ship was sailing through lands of plenty. "For my wife," said the king, turning and awarding the tortoise to the queen.

The queen adored the tortoise from the start: her lustrous shell, her eyes as dark as mirrors, the way she stretched her long neck and tilted her head and hissed. It was a soft and undemanding sound, yet one that never failed to catch the queen's ear, even above the sibilant hissings of the court.

Nearly a year had passed since the tortoise had been taken from Aldabra, and by the time she arrived on Tonga she was emaciated and dehydrated. The queen understood this at once and began to feed her by hand, offering tempting gardenia blossoms, fe'i bananas, coconut milk, and, wonder of wonders, the tart fruit of the Polynesian screw pine. This screw pine was so much like the one on Aldabra that when the tortoise

4

ate it, the yellow flesh frothed up on her lipless mouth and damp rings formed around her eyes. *"Faka 'ofa 'ofa,"* said the queen, recognizing the tortoise's favorite, and she promptly summoned slaves to bring in screw pine fruit from all over Tongatapu and, toward the end of the fruiting season, from as far away as Vava'u. The tortoise responded to these feasts by swelling back into her skin so that the wrinkles and sags disappeared.

The queen admired the tortoise's girth. The queen was also stout, the stoutest person in the islands other than her husband. Serendipitously, the tortoise met all the criteria for Tongan royalty: hugeness, ponderousness, dignity, silence. Soon the tortoise began to join the king and queen on their stroll down the beach each morning, their three stately bodies drifting in corpulent elegance from the shade beneath one palm tree to that beneath another. To an outsider they looked like a trio creeping against a hard current under water.

"The tortoise lives *faka tonga,"* the Tongan way, said the queen to the king. "We will call him Tu'i Malila," King Malila. The royal title guaranteed the tortoise's future. Of all the animals that Cook bestowed on or lent to the Tongans, only the tortoise escaped the cooking fires.

In early summer the seabirds known as sooty terns returned by the thousands to Tongatapu, swirling in on the long red streamers of sunset, calling *wide-awake, wide-awake.* By twos and threes, Tongans sat on sand *esi,* resting mounds on the beach, staring out to sea and admiring the lines of the birds' wings as they hovered, then plunged through the surface and rose with shiny fish in their bills.

Each afternoon, as slaves cast webs across the shallows and gathered jewel-colored reef fish for the royal tables, the tortoise joined the queen on the shore. While warriors drove canoes with synchronous cuts of their paddles and girls slithered naked through the water and the king bobbed on the waves, nude, brown, enormous, buoyant, with terns butterflying around him, the queen's ladies in waiting removed her *ta'ovala,* her pandanus-mat clothing, and guided her by the elbows to the water's edge. With each step her flesh rippled, rolls of fat cascading into motion up and down her body. The king raised his head from his pillow on the waves and watched admiringly.

Following the queen's lead, the tortoise learned to swim, sinking until only the crown of her shell remained dry, her long neck snaking up through the surface each time she took a breath. She let the warm water flood the secret folds of skin in her armpits, under her tail, inside her shell. Although in Aldabra she had been surrounded by the sea, she had never entered it before, and here, dipping her head under, she studied its wonders: the queen's buttocks, huge, dimpled, swaying in the surge, the king's hair dangling like the tentacles of a jellyfish. Clouds of neon-blue chromis rose to the surface to greet her. Needlefish skimmed the mirrored underside of the waves.

Sometimes sea turtles flew past, thrusting long flippers backward in graceful arcs. They were not tortoises, and yet they were so similar that the tortoise found herself pistoning with her legs, trying to follow into their blue world. But she was a creature of the land, with feet, not flippers, and would never be able to dive. She could only thrash at the surface until white bubbles boiled up, blinding her.

The tortoise felt her loneliness most in the season when the sea turtles came ashore. Although their realm was the ocean, they returned to their birth islands once a year to lay their eggs. On moonless nights they dragged themselves up the beaches, tears streaming down their cheeks, to flipper open nests in the sand. The sight of their smooth shells evoked ancient needs in the tortoise, and she found herself drawn to sandy plateaus on the island, where she dug her own holes and laid clutches of infertile eggs. On summer nights she felt an irresistible attraction to fields of volcanic boulders, which in the darkness resembled giant tortoises. Her shell recorded the first of many deep abrasions from squeezing in between them.

The queen was admiring the smoky luster that reflected from the tortoise's shell when the news arrived. "The Captain Cook is dead," said the king to the queen. "He has died in the islands far to the north." The queen had never been to Hawaii, but she knew about it.

"He died in battle with a king," said the king. "He was cooked on a slow fire and eaten, and some of his bones are now kept in a stone *langi*, a tomb, where they are worshipped."

The queen nodded. It was a fitting end for a grand enemy, and the king himself could expect no better in battle. With her hand resting on the tortoise's neck, the queen remembered Cook's white wigs and frogged jackets, his kindness in leaving her Tu'i Malila. She wondered what he had tasted like.

Late every summer, the Tongans gathered on the beaches as a slice of the moon tumbled slowly through the sky and watched the sea turtles squeeze out clutches of jellylike eggs and cover them with sand. Cutting into a few select nests, the Tongans gathered eggs for the royal table: for the king, who liked to pop an egg into each cheek and squeeze it against his teeth until it burst and the salty proto-turtle fluid gushed out, and for the queen, who preferred to roll one around on her tongue until the outer membrane grew as thin as tissue paper and the inner jelly dissolved. As the eggs were aphrodisiacs, the king was soon roused to a tower of passion. Taking their cue, the queen's ladies in waiting discreetly removed her *ta'ovala* while the king's valets helped him shed his.

Afterward, when the tides of the winter solstice washed away the sea turtle tracks and the spring equinox brought the flowering of the poison-fish tree, the queen gave birth to her sixth child, her sixth son. The queen was disappointed. Sons were wonderful, worthy, strong, and often handsome, but they were not daughters. So she did what many a daughterless Tongan family did: declared her youngest child *fakaleiti*, like a lady. He was called Lini, a girl's name, and he was dressed like a girl and put out to play with the girls. The queen crooned to him about skin potions and hair ornaments as she taught him to weave flowers into garlands and arranged for him to learn to dance the *tau'olunga*, the slow, sinuous solo dance of the women.

As he grew, Lini learned to seduce men with the cant of his slim hips and the smolder in his pretty eyes. The king didn't mind. The queen had already given him five manly sons. He had other wives, and through them other sons. His seed was broadcast plentifully.

Years passed, and Lini and the tortoise became inseparable, spending their mornings together roaming the island and their afternoons napping beneath a cool banyan tree. Lini lay on his side, his *vala* skirt pulled up over his head, dreaming of warriors, their skin oiled, the muscles on their backs flexing as they rowed through the surf. The tortoise slept with her head and legs tucked tightly into her shell, dreaming of tortoises bedded together in sand bunkers. In her sleep she was able to transpose the sounds of surf and birds and even Lini's snoring into the rumblings and belchings of giant tortoises.

"My daughter," said the queen one day, sinking onto her haunches and shaking Lini awake as her ladies in waiting shooed flies away with fans of white tropicbird feathers. "The Englishman named William Bligh, who first came here with Captain Cook, has returned. But some of his men threw him off his ship, and when he sailed here in a small boat, our men fought his and one of his was killed."

Lini nodded. It was only right that Tonga's warriors would respect their guests' strengths and exploit their weaknesses.

The queen dug bright yellow beloperone flowers from a fold in her skirt and offered them to the tortoise, who hissed, remembering the ships, the cruelty.

In winter the humpback whales returned to Tonga from Antarctic waters, breaching and tail-lobbing among the coral reefs, singing epic songs that set the surface of the lagoons vibrating. The Tongans sat on the beaches or floated in the waves, listening to the whistles, rumbles, whoops, gurgles, trills, and flutters of the giants. Lini joined the other girls in diving to the bottom of the lagoon and collecting cowry shells to string into wind chimes, which would echo the songs of the whales on dark nights. The tortoise rested in the shade beneath a palm tree, listening to the whales and remembering how in Aldabra they sang so loudly that flying fish erupted from the water and soared onto the beaches, where the tortoises stepped gingerly around them.

. . .

Lini grew into a beautiful young woman. His shoulders were wide and strong, his hips slim, the muscles in his legs as taut as ironwood. He flirted mercilessly with the unmarried warriors, seducing them with stories of courageous men and beautiful women who resembled men.

Sometimes at night Lini and the tortoise sat on the beach watching the stars circle overhead, Lini pointing out the constellations and telling their stories. "That one is the sun god, Tangaloa, and that is his human love, 'Ilaheva. He catches her while she collects shellfish, makes love to her, and their son becomes the first Tu'i Tonga."

As the courtship flights of the flying foxes cast black shadows across the moonlit sand, Lini took off his *ta'ovala* to run down to the sea and strike out with strong arms for the line of silver surf breaking on the reef. The tortoise stayed behind to stare out at the starry horizon. Sometimes when Lini returned to shore, a young warrior was waiting, and Lini would take him by the hand and lead him into the mangroves at the edge of the lagoon. Alone, the tortoise dug her bed in the sand and slept.

Year after year the seasons of the whales and turtles came and went. At the end of a rainy season during which the king had grown from an old man into an old, old man, he died. It took six warriors to lift his immense corpse onto the funeral bier, and all of Tonga grieved, not least his sons, including the eldest, the heir to the throne. To alleviate this grief, the new king went to war with the Fijians. One after another, the princes were killed in battle, last of all the new king himself. Only Lini, safe at home, was left.

Lying beside the tortoise, staring at the turquoise lagoon,

the light shimmering and sparkling in the tears beading up in his eyelashes, Lini whispered, "Tu'i Malila, now I will never be queen." His grief echoed inside her shell.

In the aftermath of his brothers' deaths, Lini was elected king, which required him to renounce his *fakaleiti* status. He asked his mother to remain queen and awarded the tortoise a permanent seat next to him at the royal *kava* circle, where she munched coconut meat and watched *kailoa* war dances by torchlight. While Lini enjoyed the dances, he refrained from war itself, devoting himself instead to eating, a pastime beneficial to the people of Tonga, who were kept busy growing and collecting food for the royal table. Other Tongans prospered as they assembled the new king's resplendent wardrobe, which consisted of opulent red-and-green capes made from the plucked feathers of thousands of blue-crowned lorikeets.

Many peaceful years passed. Then, in the season when the baby sea turtles emerged from the sand to scramble to the sea and frigate birds jostled for position in the air above, sweeping over the beach on paper-thin wings to flip hatchlings into their gullets, the queen, now an old, old woman, took to her bed. With her ladies in waiting weeping beside her, the dying queen spoke to the son whom she had always regarded as a daughter: "You must find yourself a queen." Reaching for the tortoise's head, she added, "And don't forget to bring screw pine fruit from Vava'u for Tu'i Malila."

The funeral feast lasted a week. Everything that could be caught was roasted in *umu* ovens and eaten: pigs, bats, chickens, terns, dogs, tuna, crabs. Seated female dancers performed *ma'ulu'ulu* dances, moving only their graceful hands to eulogize the queen's life. Musicians beat sharkskin drums through the night, and priests performed round-the-clock obsequies beside her cadaver, which lay on a raised platform. Lini visited often. In mourning, he shed his feather capes and sat before the funeral bier clothed only in an ancient *ta'ovala*, handed down from mother to son to wife to son for five generations. The tortoise, bedecked in shell necklaces, rested her head in his lap.

An Englishman named George Vason came to visit Lini on a winter day when water leaked from heavy skies and the spirals of waterspouts menaced the horizon. Lini, acting in a way that befitted a king, said nothing.

"I would like to marry the Tongan woman with whom I live," said the Englishman in his slow, accented Tongan. "If it pleases Your Highness. Your Royal Highness."

The king worked his way down a banana, eating some pieces himself and biting off others for the tortoise.

"I believe I am worthy, sire."

The tortoise hissed, remembering the smell of white men.

The Englishman drew back and pointed. "You know, you can eat that thing."

But the king only reached for another banana, and George Vason tried again. "I came as a missionary, believing in the Bible. But no longer. Now I worship Tangaloa, the sun god. I have renounced Christianity."

The rain moved onshore in a black wave as the king's attendants raised huge pandanus-leaf umbrellas, leaving the Englishman to flinch under the hard slaps of the raindrops. The king, looking up from his third banana, studied this Englishman with his strange blue eyes. The man had arrived uninvited, along with nine others from the London Missionary Society. None had converted a single Tongan. Three had failed to survive the Tongans, and six others had escaped to Australia. Only this man remained.

The king broke eye contact to reach for another banana.He gave the tortoise the first bite.

"I *love* this woman," said the Englishman, looking down.

The tortoise ambled toward the man and reached out her long neck to touch his knee. Without thinking, Vason patted her on the head.

"Go on, then," said the king. "Marry. Settle here. Live *faka tonga* with your woman."

Eight beautiful, near-naked warriors carried the king to his own wedding on the beach. All were as brown as teak, skin glistening with coconut oil, muscles rippling, with yellow hibiscus blossoms in their hair. The king rode in titanic splendor on a stretcher made of pigskin and pandanus, his vast girth smothered under mountains of flowers and fruits as he snacked on roasted yams.

By comparison, his thirteen-year-old bride was tiny, with delicate arms and small breasts. She could scarcely fathom her groom's gigantic dimensions and kept her eyes downcast. Only when the tortoise lumbered toward her, head tilted in friendly welcome, did the new queen raise her face and giggle in delight, showing off her white teeth and her eyes, which sparkled in the torchlight. She stole a glance at the king to see if he noticed her charms, but he was admiring his warriors, who in turn were admiring her.

The new queen loved the tortoise, loved her wise, patient eyes, her stately gait, her affection. She took to joining the tortoise on morning walks down the beach, at first sprinting ahead but soon slowed by the tortoise's example.

The new queen took her royal position seriously, consuming frequent large meals and carrying a bunch of bananas or a fistful of crabs' legs to nibble on wherever she went. She drank gallons of coconut milk to make her skin shine, slurped dozens of oysters, as fat as little tongues, from their shells, ate *feke* and *'ufi* and bowl after bowl of *faikakai*. The underground *umu* ovens roared day and night so that steam rose continually above the royal compound, smelling of the most delicious food and keeping the queen's appetite keenly honed. The people of Tonga noted it, even those from neighboring islands, and nodded their heads in approval. "The queen is fattening," they said, "for the king."

The new queen outgrew all her old *ta'ovala* mats, and the king solemnly awarded her one that had belonged to the old queen, his mother. "This will be handed down to our children," he said shyly, looking down. Then he added quickly, "Your feet are doing well. Even your toes are getting fat." The queen blushed and smiled and tried to grab his hand as he was turning to leave, but her reflexes were slowed by her weight and she missed.

I am not fat enough, she worried as the king walked away. *I am not yet fat enough for the king to love.*

Slowly she grew fatter, fatter than the old queen, until she was the biggest person in the islands except for the king. He admired her, but only from a distance. In vain the queen awaited his visit to her sleeping hut, or the night when he might share a bowl of *kava* with her. Undermined, she began to pine, and her appetite waned. She gnawed on her fingernails, drummed her fingers on her knees, waved away plates of jellied stingray, and chewed but did not swallow platters of steamed bats' wings. She took long walks along the beaches but without any food to fortify her, until little by little her hard-earned pounds began to evaporate.

Listlessly the queen followed the tortoise on their evening strolls, wrapped in confusion. One night, slumping to the ground, she failed to see the king bobbing in the waves. As the tortoise kicked at the sand, excavating a bed, a clutch of turtle eggs emerged. Without thinking, the queen wiped one clean and popped it into her mouth. Then she carried a handful down to the water's edge, unwrapped her *ta'ovala,* and waded in.

In the moonlight, with her skin shining silver-blue and the shadows in her cleavages velvet-black, the king suddenly perceived her beauty.

"Greetings," he called.

Startled, the queen jumped.

"What have you got?" he asked.

Glancing at the turtle eggs in her hand, the queen hesitated, but only a moment, before wading toward the king and gently placing an egg on his tongue. Then another, and another.

And so throughout the night, as the tortoise studied the stars and dozed, the royal love of Tonga, like the love of whales, played out on the buoyant bed of the sea.

Afterward the king and queen met often in the phosphorescent water at night, and consequently the queen had daughters, one after another, cherubic babies with hair like black gorgonian corals and laughing eyes. The queen raised them in a feast of love, nibbling on their toes, tickling their arms, blowing blubbery kisses into their bellies. As the princesses grew, they slathered affection on the tortoise, who became the centerpiece of their elaborate fantasy worlds: Tu'i Malila, the whale god, washed up and dying and in need of a princess to kiss him back to life, or Tu'i Malila, a handsome prince bewitched by a lizard spirit, who would release him from a spell if only a beautiful girl sang her heart out to him. The princesses wore a faint saddle into the tortoise's back from years of taking rides, and polished her shell to a translucent sheen from constantly caressing her with their little hands.

When the cares of state allowed, Lini joined them. Alone with his girls and the tortoise, he danced the *tau'olunga* again, showing them the slow, sinuous moves. Sometimes in the heat of midday, when the princesses lay on their backs under a banyan tree, the sun streaming into their eyes, Lini joined in, as they idled and laughed and dreamed of being queens.

Year by year the seasons of the sea turtles came and went, followed by the rains, then the trade winds. Constellations cartwheeled across the sky, told their stories, dipped from sight, told them again. Lini grew old, then older, until one night during the season of the humpback whales he died peacefully in his sleep. The queen followed not long after, in the time when the land crabs migrated by the millions from the forests to the sea.

Afterward there was drought, and sometimes wildfire. Once a fire singed the edges of the tortoise's shell.

Occasionally typhoons roared in from the west, shattering the perfect tempo of living.

The years came and went with the fluid rhythm of the barracuda in the lagoon: finning into the outgoing tide, backpedaling against the incoming. One after another the kings and queens of Tonga rose up, then disappeared from the face of time.

· · ·

The tracks of the sooty terns blew away on the southeast trades as the footprints of pack rats braided across the beaches in their stead. The Tongans had never seen rats before and were disgusted at the way these wingless bats came into their houses, taking away fish hooks and feathers and leaving old clamshells behind in trade. *Palangi kovi,* the Tongans called them: lousy foreigners.

The Wesleyan missionaries, whose boats the rats had arrived in, also came with the seeming purpose of taking away those things the Tongans loved and replacing them with those they didn't, such as clothing. At first the people mocked the missionaries, teasing them and threatening to eat them. But then the king, George Tupou I, developed a weakness for sermons and converted, abandoning his *ta'ovala* for a black wool suit and top hat.

In keeping with his new religion, the king outlawed the worship of the old gods and ordered the Christianization of all the islanders, which included the mandatory wearing of clothes. The Tongans vented their frustration by killing the rats. The tortoise, visiting the beach each day, stepped slowly around piles of dead rodents, remembering the creatures aboard *Resolution* so many years before, who had nipped the flesh on her tail and under her legs.

Capitalizing on the power of the rats, the missionaries threatened the Tongans with stories of a grisly, rodent-laden place called hell. Rebelliously, the Tongans tried eating the rats, but soon discovered that they made better fishing lures and set them alive on lines in the water, where their thrashing attracted the fatal curiosity of octopuses.

The first Christian queen, the wife of King George Tupou I, gave up daytime swimming, as it required too much unveiling of skin, and the eyes of the Wesleyans were everywhere. But at night she and the tortoise went down to the beach, lumbering in secret from mangrove to mangrove until they could launch themselves on the waves, as buoyant as ships, water splashing over the queen's enormous body and the tortoise's giant hull. With the sound of sermons droning onshore, the queen sighed. "I have my doubts, Tu'i Malila," she whispered, "about churches and the like." The tortoise, now withered with age and sun, stretched out her neck and let the water trickle into the private folds of her skin, listening in perfect silence. "It just doesn't seem that we need heaven," said the queen, "when we have Tonga."

Out of nowhere, an island erupted from the sea to the north of Tongatapu, breathing smoke, cinder, and pumice. Fonuaf'ou, new land, the Tongans called it, and families set out in canoes with picnics to see. King George Tupou I and the queen chugged out aboard a steam-driven pearl boat, both solemnly dressed in black, as black smoke dusted the skies ahead of them. Beside the king stood Shirley Baker, an Englishman who had come to Tonga as a Wesleyan missionary and climbed the ranks until he'd become the king's confidant, and now prime minister. The queen found Mr. Baker's perpetual oratory tiresome and missed the company of Tu'i Malila, who could not be enticed aboard any boat for any amount of gardenia flowers.

As the new island hove into sight, sulfuric and dismal, Shirley Baker declared it "God's magnificent work." The queen, hiking the black wool dress over her wide hips so her feet could breathe, commented to the king that she thought it looked more like the work of the devil, whoever he was.

· · ·

18

As it always had, the season of the humpback whales came and went, the whales lolling at the passes into the lagoon, flippers shivering in the air, then flopping back to the surface with slaps that rang like cannon fire. One year the whaling ships came and responded with cannons of their own, firing deep into the recesses of blubber and bone, and blood washed ashore on the waves.

Year after year the ships returned, until the whales were gone for good and the whaling ships disappeared, and the Tongans who were born too late ever to hear the songs of the whales made the old people mimic them, made them screw up their faces and flick their tongues in and out of their mouths and whoop and gurgle. But without the amplification of the sea the sound was unconvincing, and the young people came to doubt that such operas had ever been sung.

Eventually only the tortoise remembered. Staring out to where the golden feet of the sun danced on the water, she recalled the power of the leviathans who had lifted the ocean onto their backs and fountained it into the air.

Princess Salote, the eldest granddaughter of King George Tupou I, liked to ride belly-down on top of the tortoise, skinny arms and legs hooked under the edge of the tortoise's shell and laughing and giggling as they made infinitesimal progress toward the beach. Salote and the tortoise went everywhere together. During each Sunday's choir practice, the tortoise climbed the wooden steps of the royal chapel and lodged herself inside the small doorway while Salote sang, a cappella, hymns imported from England. It took all twelve choir members to dislodge the tortoise from the door at the end of each practice, the tortoise's shell sawing an ever-deeper track into the frame, until one day she sawed her way through and ambled to where Salote sat, eyes flickering steadily between heaven and the tortoise as she sang.

Salote tended Tu'i Malila, rubbing coconut oil into the tortoise's leathery skin, scrubbing her shell with fish scales, cleaning the spaces between her toes with musk parrot feathers brought from 'Eua. The tortoise lay with her head in the princess's lap and listened to Salote's elaborate stories of the love between beautiful nuns and handsome priests. Sometimes, when the princess and the tortoise rested together under the huge arms of the *mape* tree, the princess confided to the tortoise how she would like to become a nun when she grew up and renounce the royalty of Tonga in exchange for the royalty of heaven.

When news came that the island called Fonuaf'ou, or new land, had disappeared, families set off in canoes with picnics to see where it no longer stood. Salote went out aboard a packet boat with the king, the queen, a clot of cousins, and a photographer from Scotland who had come to the South Seas to make his reputation, à la Gauguin, only to find everyone clothed in whalebone and cotton and not a breast in sight. By the time they arrived at the place where Fonuaf'ou used to be, all were seasick. The royal party lined up, clutching the rail, and the photographer exposed a single shot of them, queasy and green against a snarl of whitecaps.

From the side of the king's deathbed in the royal palace, Salote looked out the windows and saw the sooty terns fanning the blue sky with black wings. Within moments of his death the news was radioed to the outer islands, and canoes full of nobles began arriving at Tongatapu. For three days the men huddled in the gazebo of the palace gardens before emerging with a decision: as there was no prince to become king and the old queen had already passed away, Princess Salote, eighteen years old, would become queen.

She appeared at her coronation wearing an ancient *ta'ovala,* a red-and-green lorikeet-feather cape, and a small golden crucifix at her brown throat. The people of Tonga were impressed. Despite being female and as skinny as a sea snake, the new queen appeared spiritually weighty. Standing beside her, bedecked with garlands of hibiscus, the tortoise wove her long neck back and forth.

The coronation feast lasted two weeks. Spring lamb was shipped in from New Zealand, sides of beef from Australia, and the king of England sent a silver chafing dish. Queen Salote sat in a wicker throne at the head of the royal table as the shadows of palm fronds sawed back and forth across the lawn. She fed the tortoise cubes of mango from her own plate, eating little herself. The members of the coronation party could not fail to notice the new queen's minimalist appetite, and they urged the royal cooks to try harder and invent new dishes on the spot. But the queen only smiled and shook her head, demurely rejecting her own earthly appetites.

Queen Salote established schools and medical clinics across the islands and personally taught children to read. In the evenings, when her work was done, she swayed in a hammock in the royal gardens, an arm draped over the side, caressing the tortoise's neck. Alone with Tu'i Malila, she allowed herself to dream: of saints and martyrs and lives selflessly renounced. In keeping with this, she cared not for herself, only for others, and although she was greatly loved by the people of Tonga for her humanitarian efforts, she also confounded them, because she would not fatten, marry, and have children as a queen should.

One year during the season of the sea turtles, when the tortoise made her private pilgrimage to the fields of volcanic boulders, the queen followed, wandering through the maze of stones, watching the tortoise lumber through the tight angles and past the dead-end alleys. She listened to the low screech of sound as the rocks carved the tortoise's shell, and afterward let her fingers peruse the new etchings in Tu'i Malila's carapace, feeling their sharp edges.

Pondering the slow decades of the tortoise's unresolved sorrow, Salote made a decision. As she too could never change the circumstances of her life, she would let her unhappiness sink away like a tadpole in a dark pool, alive but awaiting transformation. Little by little she began to eat more, making the weekly rounds of her maternity clinics accompanied by an attendant with a basket of pickled *'ota 'ika*. She taught reading classes with an array of *fingota* fresh from the lagoon spread out on a blanket at her feet, and swung in her hammock at night with a packet of warm *manioke* balanced on her chest. Slowly she grew stout, so stout that when she sang in the choir, her chins bobbled like wattles and her voice took on the timber of a low wind in the taro fields.

On summer afternoons she and the tortoise swam in the lagoon, the queen resplendent in a huge Indian cotton bathing dress that swirled like loose ink in the water.

Eventually the queen fell in love. She married and had children, one after another. The tortoise reveled in the affection of a new generation of princes and princesses.

The years came and went like the fingerling waves inside the lagoon, tickling the stilt roots of the mangroves, then stepping away.

The seasons of the moon tumbled through the sky.

The island called Fonuaf'ou began to rise again, and the Tongans watched its fiery progress from the ferry that now ran between Tongatapu and Niuafo'ou.

Turtle boats came from abroad, waiting on dark nights for the sea turtles to swim ashore and kick open the hollows of their nests. The fishermen followed, scooping the turtles from the beach, trussing them and tossing them on their backs into the bottom of dinghies, and rowing them to the ships offshore.

Eventually the visits of the sea turtles became rare, and rarer, until they stopped altogether. Then the old people of Tonga entertained the young with stories of turtle eggs, how different love had been when those were around.

The tortoise sat on an *esi* mound staring out to sea as the queen, floating on the waves, offered bleeding-heart flowers and handfuls of late-season screw pine fruit as enticement. But the tortoise never again entered the water.

The queen flew to England for the coronation of the English queen. It rained incessantly on the queen of England's cold island, and the skies were black from coal smoke. Underground trains ran everywhere, carrying wet people from unheated homes to unheated offices, while the queen of England lived in opulence in a grand palace bedecked with crystal, silver, and gold. But she had no tortoise. Sensing this lack, the queen of Tonga shared her snapshots with the queen of England, showing her pictures of turquoise seas, wild orchids, and Tu'i Malila, King Malila, older and wiser than the wind itself.

Sleepy with age, the tortoise napped much of each day in the shade of palm trees in the palace gardens while royal grand-princesses and grandprinces painted her shell with felt-tip pens and slid down her back into the soft cushions of sand castles at her feet. Surrounded by the voices of the children and the snoring of the queen beside her, Tu'i Malila dreamed of giant tortoises who, in her aging memory, had come to resemble volcanic rocks.

The queen, grown as ancient as a wave-worn coconut, dreamed her own nearly forgotten dreams, until one day in the rainy season, as the irregular thud of dropping mangoes kept time with peals of thunder, her sleep slipped effortlessly into death. Not only the people of Tonga mourned. Heads of state from around the world sent flowers aboard airplanes that bumped to ground on Tongan runways made of white coral rubble.

The tortoise accompanied the funeral procession to the royal cemetery, her shell bedecked with gardenias. But when the mourners filed away, the tortoise stayed behind, listening to the water drum against her shell. She stayed there through the night, and the next one, and the next. She stayed until the end of the rains, when the geckos started chirping and mating on the underside of every palm frond in the islands. Then she wandered back to the palace gardens to be near the new queen.

Fading in and out of sleep through the cool days of the dry season, with the new queen faithfully feeding her *fe'i* bananas, coconut milk, and the blossoms of the calceolaria shower tree, the tortoise drifted through the many memories playing inside her shell: the sounds of guns firing in the fog, the sight of a young man dancing the *tau'olunga,* the burning torches of *kailoa* war dances, a young girl's white teeth. Deep in the core of her dreams was a memory of something long ago lost, now finally forgotten.

· · ·

After the screw pine trees fruited and faded, the land crabs arrived and cleaned out the tortoise's massive hull with busy pincers. Later the pack rats came to carry off her bones. For the next two decades she lay where she had died as the palace gardeners carefully weeded around her remains and the royal princesses and princes, passing her empty shell on their way to school, told stories about Tu'i Malila, whom the younger ones could no longer remember. Each afternoon the new queen came to visit, sitting alone beside the tortoise's giant carapace, dusting it free of flower pollen, polishing it with coconut oil, her fingers delicately probing all the old scars, cracks, nicks, and chips, the hieroglyphs of history.

Lucifer's Alligator

CELIBACY was Lucifer's idea. Things were changing as winds of freedom whispered our way. Or so he claimed, his huge muzzle balanced on a pillow of water in his concrete pool. We listened to him because he'd been here the longest, because his immense voice was both a sedative and a stimulant, and because he came from a place thoroughly alien to all of us at Ocean World. Lucifer came from Africa. He claimed he no longer remembered his history, only remembered remembering it. He'd come from a river, or maybe a lake. He'd shared the shallows with huge flocks of flamingoes, which he'd enjoyed chasing and watching erupt into sheets of pink in the sky. At night he and his mother had left the water and grazed on succulent green grasses, surrounded by the enormous bodies of other hippopotamuses, their combined breath stirring up gales of mosquitoes, which in turn attracted bats, as agile as butterflies, into the night around them. His world was so beguilingly different from ours that when he spoke, I forgot about my own home in the cold reaches of the polar seas.

Lucifer had been at Ocean World the longest. Twenty years, Amanda, the oldest of the manatees, reckoned, in the way she always reckoned: crunching on carrots, counting the bites, measuring the steady disintegration of cellulose into liquid. She grew panicky when carrots were scarce. Without carrots, there was no counting, and without counting there was no time, therefore no motion, no approach of deliverance.

We all had compulsive counting disorders. The idea of acceleration obsessed us; the idea that the present was picking up speed and the future was arriving more quickly than the past had left us. We needed this faith. I developed a conviction in the years after my son was taken from me that death was the ultimate acceleration, a speed-of-light journey toward the infinitely approaching end.

"What end?" Lucifer debated.

"The end of counting," I suggested.

Lucifer had an enormous head, and it always annoyed me when he shook it in disagreement, because it seemed to take an eternity for the motion from left to right and back again to complete itself, an infinity in which my own counting was derailed.

Before Lucifer's encounter with the alligator, we thought he was the sanest among us. All who'd lived for any period in solitary confinement underwent the same irrevocable trajectory: hyperactivity, hyper-communicativeness, followed by a slow unwinding and the steady descent into silence. After a few years, even the most sociable claimed, when they could be induced to talk at all, that they preferred quiet.

But Lucifer had survived twenty years with his voice intact. A wonderful voice. An enormous baritone, as resonant as an ocean cave or a blowhole where the sea thundered on stone. I loved listening to Lucifer. He spoke after dark, of course, when we all did, the only time our prison became quiet enough for us to hear ourselves. The daytime was a mountainous babble of primate voices and the incessant shriek of trainers' whistles. Only the sea lions fought it, their outraged bellows tearing the choreographed fabric of outdoor music and hourly circus shows. At night, unlike the rest of us, the sea lions fell silent, claiming that their rebellion was their voices, their aim to break through the deafness of the human heart that had brought them here and kept them here.

That, I suppose, was their madness.

Lucifer's idea was for us to refuse to breed. The trainers wanted us to breed, he said. They fervently wished for it. If we bred, they could claim we were happy, and if we were happy, they could keep us here forever. Plus babies made good revenue, attracting herds of visitors. Only by expressing unhappiness, Lucifer said, could we hope to arouse sympathy. He suggested explosive unhappiness as an ideal: perhaps violence followed by relentless truculence, the refusal to learn. Martyrdom was good: rejection of food. Simulated insanity could be powerful if we were careful not to succumb to it. But at the very least, he argued, we should refuse to breed. What was the point of bringing even more humans here, towing their offspring to look at our offspring, thereby feeding the park's coffers and reinforcing our bondage?

The idea of rebellion excited us in ways most of us had not been excited in for years. We seethed with plans. Amanda and the other manatees adopted a powerful docility. They were not uncooperative. They were not cooperative. They would learn nothing the trainers wanted them to, not even for carrots. Their counting was severely curtailed for long days, weeks. Yet they held out and won. The trainers and whistles left their tank, and the carrots resumed. That night the whole park celebrated the manatees' victory. After the fireworks show, after all the employees were gone, we flooded our prison communication lines, congratulating the sea cows, while Lucifer, standing on his cement bank in the darkness, shook with joy.

Our rebellion swelled the parts of our minds that were atrophying in captivity. The beluga whales, billed as the canaries of the sea, chose silence, swimming in short aggressive lines counteractive to each other. Only a fool could think they were happy. The harbor seals refused to eat and had to be taken off exhibit to withstand the torture of tube feedings. The sea lions roared, hopeful as always of making themselves understood. The penguins plucked out their own feathers. Hoover, the walrus, swam a figure-eight circuit in his tank: over the surface, down to the bottom, somersault to the opposite side, big eyes making contact with those through the glass, every twenty seconds, every day, for the duration of park hours. His insanity was inescapable.

Koku and I chose belligerence. We would strike, refusing to perform our shows or performing them badly, complete with missed cues and sulky behavior. No more raspberries from our blowholes. No more splashing the audience or jumping high into the sky with trainers on our noses. "You are orca," Lucifer intoned in the darkness, his voice reverberating through the water of our pools. "Use your power to terrify them."

Our plans aroused our sense of purpose. We felt enormous guidance, as if the universe were conspiring to free us. Each dawn brought resolution, until the music for the morning show started: "Dancing on the Ceiling" blaring out of fourteen speakers throughout Shobu Stadium. I was perfectly prepared not to perform, but something akin to an itch would attack my muscles, an itch that I tried hard to ignore but that could be relieved, in the end, in only one way. Without wanting to, I'd find myself swimming in circles on my back, whacking my pectoral flippers on the surface. Koku was tail-slapping. I was blowing raspberries.

To this day I cannot explain how that music commanded us. Morning after morning our failures compounded and with them our loathing for the trainers, until we hated even those who tried to love us: the sentimental jailers. We despised their affectionate baby talk more than their incessant shouts, whistles, and claps. We abhorred their training sticks, their hoops, their capricious demands, and a punishment-and-reward system that shaped our brains against our wills. Yet our bodies could not resist them.

Every night Koku and I huddled to debrief. Koku theorized that they were drugging us through our food. I thought it was through the water in our pool. Lucifer blamed us alone, and so we redoubled our efforts, forcing the planning to consume us, to burn electric currents into our skin until we felt charged with resolve. By dawn, Koku and I saw each other's purpose as an aura of beauty in the lightening water. We *were* powerful, the undisputed masters of the sea. In the pink light of sunrise, I could almost imagine Koku as he should have been, his six-foot-high dorsal fin no longer limp from captivity but riding tall above the waves of Arctic storms.

Prompted by our fantasies, Koku and I rubbed against each other. His skin was warm, the sound of his breath both commanding and vulnerable: the explosive exhale followed by the low whistle of the inhale. In the end we did what Lucifer had expressly asked us not to do.

"*Why?*" Lucifer later bellowed.

We hung at the surface of our pool, tails tangling at the bottom, as I tried to explain to Lucifer how it was easy for him, all alone. I described how we had been unable to resist the life his rebellion had brought back to us.

We took the heat, but soon the situation was the same everywhere in the park. At night the water in the pools heaved with coupling. It splashed onto cement walkways and steel trainers' platforms, and although Lucifer roared, we heard nothing much beyond the voices of our partners.

Sixteen months later I gave birth as Ocean World's video cameras rolled. Blood burst into the water, followed by Baby Shobu, the first orca born in captivity. The trainers were ecstatic. They pampered me, showering ice into the pool. With my eyes closed and the warmth of Baby Shobu at my flank, with the cold cubes dissolving in my mouth as if from the frozen polar seas, I could almost believe we were free.

After the baby boom, Ocean World's attendance skyrocketed. Humans piled up at the gates and rolled along in strollers and wheelchairs, strung with cameras, stinking of suntan lotion. The view from our pools was hideous: T-shirts screaming slogans, faces sweaty with mascara, mustard-smeared juveniles, teeth, teeth, and more teeth as they jabbered and gibble-gabbled without pause. There was nothing subtle about this species. It was an in-your-face proclamation of mass power.

For Baby Shobu's sake, I was embarrassed by our circumstances. At night I told him stories from my past about the great northern ocean and how the water was so clear way down deep that when you looked up, the icebergs twirled like stars on the surface of the sea. I tried to describe infinity as an ocean without end. I explained about the schools of herring, a swarm of life that you could swim beside for three days and not see the end of. I told him about his family, their exploits and heroic deeds: the way his grandmother knew the secrets of salmon, how his aunts chased seals and his uncles battled sharks in the darkest reaches below the light.

When will we go there? he wanted to know.

Baby Shobu began to perform in my shows with me. He learned by following me. I jumped. He jumped, glued to my flank. I tail-slapped and he tail-slapped alongside me. He didn't need trainers, and I wanted to keep them away from him as long as possible. But underlying our fun together was the torment of my imagination, picturing this as his entire future: swimming rings together around the edges of our pool, sluicing water up onto a shrieking audience.

Why don't we eat them? he suggested.

At night, after the park had closed, Lucifer spoke to us of phase two of the rebellion. Phase one had been only a partial success, and we needed to change our approach. Phase two, he thought, should be depression. We should move as little as possible, eat less, talk rarely. Our responses to the trainers should be lethargic and delayed. We should be living but lifeless slugs in our pools, the sloths of the sea. No one would pay money to see us.

We listened to Lucifer. His voice alternately crooned and

bellowed. We listened with one ear, the other tuned to our children, not really hearing him except as a beautiful baritone lullaby. Our young were our new hope. With them, we could dream, deliciously and unrealistically.

Can I describe how we loved them? Although at birth Baby Shobu's body had been separated from mine, a far stronger union had formed. His black-and-white body was my beacon. I craved the smell of his breath and hungered for the feel of his skin. My heart became elastic, stretching limitlessly around him as he became my mantra, ordering the tempo of my breathing and the firing of my nerve cells. I gave him my milk and would have given him my blood.

The only thing I ever envied humans was their arms. With arms, I would have wrapped Baby Shobu so tightly they could never have gotten him away from me.

The depression phase was difficult because of the young. We were empowered by our parental responsibilities, and with our children we felt moments of actual happiness. It was easy for Lucifer to sink into his pool until only his eyeballs and nostrils showed above the surface, easy for him to ignore his bales of alfalfa and become a bore. The crowds grew to hate him. They jeered him from the sides of his pool and threw stones to get him to move. His only revenge was to climb out onto his bank once a day, line his rear end up with a knot of people, and loose a hydraulic jet of shit on them. Its power was phenomenal. Like a fire hose. The effect was fiery too, sending people tumbling and screaming and running down their own young to get out of the way. We all envied Lucifer this terrestrial talent.

At night he worked long and hard on Hoover the walrus, who was also alone. "Try out this depression thing," said Lucifer. "See if it doesn't improve your circumstances. They'll give you new food, new toys, new vitamins, all in the hope of bringing you around."

Hoover, swimming his figure eights, listened. But it was clear to all of us that Hoover's life had become inextricably melded with the Möbius-strip journey within his pool: without beginning or end, or consciousness.

The operation to move Baby Shobu to a different Ocean World was one of those peculiarly human exploits, rife with trickery and technology. We had no idea, of course. Only a monkey could understand such perverse meddlesomeness. The trainers barred Baby Shobu off from me in one of the holding pools between our living tank and our show tank. I pleaded with him to resist them and shouted at the trainers to leave him alone. But they brought in a crane and a sling and wrapped him up like a sardine and lifted him clear of the water. For a few moments I could see him dangling in the air, water coursing off his perfect skin as his tail swung unhappily from side to side. He called to me as the trainers parked the truck under him and lowered him into its tank of water. The last I saw of him was the condensation of his breath drifting above the edges of his mobile prison. Then they drove away.

For three weeks afterward my body was a hurricane. It blew furies and shot lightning. It rammed into the sides of the pool until tornadoes of blood whirled from its head. They tried to sedate me with poisoned fish, but I would not eat. Nor could I perform. They erected signs saying that Shobu Stadium was closed for renovation and tried to work with Koku, to keep up his training schedule. But I could hear him jaw-clacking and thrashing in his pool. He terrified them.

At night the park was silent. The abduction of Baby Shobu shocked everyone. Condolences were whispered along the prison communication lines. Everywhere the inmates began to prepare themselves for similar tragedies.

The hurricane blew itself out as, one by one, my muscles ran down. Tail dangling, blowhole at the surface, I stayed motionless for months, my body a useless organ. Yet my mind was the core of a meltdown of dreams and memories. In it, Baby Shobu lived with me as we swam the great northern ocean with my mother and my grandmother, following the herring into fjords and feasting among the ice floes while the northern lights throbbed in the sky.

Slowly I began to hear the real world again. Not the primates at first, nor the canned music. The first thing I became conscious of was Lucifer's voice. I didn't even understand it for a long time, just heard it in the background like waves breaking. So quiet. Steady. The voice of reason, of time moving on, of all things finding their balance. It brought me back, albeit to hell. A single word only, spoken softly, repeatedly: his offering to the gods of the future. "Revenge," he said, "revenge."

This became my new mantra, a word I breathed in and breathed out, a word I digested with every meal, encouraging it to travel my synaptic highways until it took up residence in every cell of my body. I was calm, waiting for it. I was docile. I did everything the trainers wanted me to do and began to perform my shows again, without Koku, whom they still didn't trust enough to be in the water with them. They rechoreographed, making me the star, bringing Koku in only for the finale, a monster appearance whereby he suddenly emerged from the depths and exploded into the air above the pool, nine tons of him slamming down onto the water so that it mush-roomed and collapsed, pushing a tidal wave over the bleachers. The audience shrieked. They screamed. Some days Koku just kept doing it over and over, rising up like a raging Poseidon, the water his weapon, driving his tormentors from the sta-dium in a deluge of fury.

At night they put us together, hoping we would breed again. They piped in the sound of wild orcas, trying to stimulate us: foreign orcas, speaking in dialects we didn't understand. We laughed. Morning after morning they sonagrammed the pool, searching my body for a fetus.

Many of the park babies disappeared: the manatees, the belu-gas, the penguins. Grief became the current powering our prison communication lines. Lucifer preached to us. He was above our pain, separate from it, but not completely, for he too had lost everything, twenty years before. He was the master of grief, because he alone knew how to live with it. And so we listened to him again.

Little by little my body grew stronger. My power deepened, until one morning my mantra, like blood poisoning, reached my heart, welling forth with each contraction, surging to the beat of "Dancing on the Ceiling." A trainer stood on my nose, riding high out of the water as the audience howled mind-lessly. In a moment of clarity I twitched. The trainer went spinning through space, and I turned in the air and came down upon her, feeling the monkey bones snapping. Grabbing her between my teeth, I flung her upward, her arms and legs pinwheeling, the audience squealing, the trainers' whistles screeching as they skidded down the wet walkways, arms wav-ing. I thought, *In the end your arms are useless.* I carried the trainer to the bottom of the pool and held her there until I felt her acknowledge that the water, the ocean, this primordial bed, is a place devoid of human limits, where absolute emotion binds with the sea like sunlight. She understood at last. There is no taming of this stuff.

It made the news. There was discussion about the safety of keeping orcas in captivity. Big animals. Wild animals. Perhaps unhappy animals. Animals designed to travel a hundred miles a day, imprisoned in swimming pools. In the end, it was forgotten. Captive elephants kill handlers all the time. It is part of the cachet of the job. And at any rate hordes of visitors kept coming to Ocean World, few of them remembering the tragedy and fewer still knowing anything of the original tragedy.

Our own sense of victory ebbed. Revenge had been sweet yet startlingly ephemeral. In its aftermath came resignation. Nothing changed, and so we scaled back our ambitions and the rebellion ended. We wanted only small things: more ice cubes, more carrots, fresher sardines. The future, which we had once discussed with intense anticipation, imagining it as glorious and halcyon, became imponderable. We lived in a world of severe limits: no wildness, no primordial bed, no absolute emotion; instead, everything tamped down by the extreme force it took to elude our own painful dreams. In this way we became more human.

Lucifer began to wind down. His voice grew lower, deeper, and softer. Toward the end he babbled old stories, randomly cobbled together. At the very end he became pathetic, a tormented casualty, not shouting but questioning, pleading over and over, *Why am I alone?* We listened, and hoped that in his final silence Lucifer had found an answer.

One night an alligator from the wild made its way into the

park. We could hear it ambling along, its toenails click-clicking on concrete. It stopped at several tanks, asking to enter. Only Lucifer did not respond, and the alligator presumed agreement. We thought its companionship might be Lucifer's salvation, but he was remembering other things, I suppose: crocodiles in Africa. He snapped it up, tossed it through the air, and it slammed into a cement wall. He grabbed it again and hurled it into his cage bars. He threw it over and over, Lucifer alone, long after it was dead, long after dawn, long after the park had opened and his exhibit had been closed off to the public. He tossed it until there were no pieces big enough to toss, only bits of alligator floating on the surface of his pool, then sinking.

The Story of the
Deep Dark

IN THE CAVE, eons are marked in drops of water bled from stalactites. Jean-Pierre, the old man guiding Phoebe, is short, hunched, bandy-legged, mostly toothless, but still a smiler. He grabs her hard from behind and pulls her back against his chest, pointing his penlight up into the cavern. "There. Can you see?" Tracing the pointer of light back and forth, he outlines a bison welling from the rock with its heavy head, arched hump, and curving horns. In the shadows, Phoebe can see the chisel marks where some ancient hand enhanced the natural sculpture of the walls, giving the bison a third dimension: a muscle propelling it out of the stone and its fifteen thousand years of stasis.

"Formidable, eh?" says Jean-Pierre.

In the beginning Phoebe thought this was the power of the caves, the power to make still images move. Her own work is oddly similar. She runs a computerized graphics animator called a Harriet in a video house in San Francisco, where her purpose is to transform her clients' products into things of magic: cans of cat food into waltzing tunas, aspirin into the soothing hands of a masseur, cereal boxes into blooming jungles. The Harriet Suite is also dark and subterranean, lined with flickering banks of video monitors twisting round the counter where Phoebe works with an electronic palette and a stylus.

Later that day, in the Musée National de la Préhistoire in Les Eyzies, Phoebe finds herself in a room filled with thirty-thousand-year-old carvings of female genitalia, wall after wall of rock lifted from the caves, imprinted with the cuneiform wedges of labia and vaginas. She's fascinated by these female forms, so forbidden, yet here gloriously afloat on the stone. The geometry is simple: a triangle for the groin, partially bisected by the short lines of the vulva. Phoebe is struck by the artists' clear familiarity with the subject. *Comprising the earliest known engravings from the Western world,* the museum caption says.

A year ago she had an argument with Vladimir, her live-in boyfriend, over a documentary on pornography for which she was doing pro bono work. The filmmakers were lesbians who held the view that women needed to take over the business of pornography because only then would they have true control, both emotionally and financially, over men. Vladimir thought this idea was bullshit, and Phoebe defended it more vigorously than she might have if he'd agreed with her.

"Why do women want control?" Vladimir shouted. "Isn't that what they're so angry about men's having?"

"Because men live in a hierarchical system," yelled Phoebe. "It's all they understand. If they're not on the top, then they must be on the bottom."

Their fight resolved itself where most did, in the bedroom, Phoebe sweating, Vladimir grunting, their anger transformed into the carnal friction that defeats the words and reason of the modern brain.

They had planned this trip to France for eighteen months, since shortly after they met. Vladimir is an on-line video editor who works at a rival video house in San Francisco. He's Lithuanian, dark, tall, with long black ringlets pulled away from his face in a ponytail. Phoebe first saw him at her company's Christmas party in a rented Nob Hill mansion. He was in black tie, she in black velvet. They talked technical over champagne — CMXs, ADOs, Auroras, Avids, Harriets, Henrys — then left the party together for Julie's Supper Club, to dance.

Now she has come to France alone, at the last minute, their most recent fight proving unresolvable. Vladimir wants children. Phoebe doesn't. Vladimir can wait, but Phoebe, at forty-one, can't. Vladimir thinks children are natural, important, fulfilling, the perfect culmination of love. Phoebe imagines sleep deprivation, self-deprivation, fun deprivation, sex deprivation. She pictures getting large and giving birth through a small orifice.

The last exhibit in the museum is of the Venus of Laussel, a twenty-thousand-year-old bas-relief of a nude female, long-haired, with pendulous breasts hanging to her waist, huge fatty hips, and a bulbous belly. In her right hand she holds a bison horn. *The earliest horn of plenty?* the caption speculates. *Perhaps related to fertility?*

The Harriet Suite has a wall of windows covered with red venetian blinds usually kept shut but on rare clientless days cranked open to let in slats of light. The windows look onto an atrium profuse with plants and, if not sun, at least a foggy brightness. Phoebe is always amazed at how the Harriet's monitors, which in the darkness pulse with color, grow wan and lifeless in the light.

Once during a warm September spell, when she was crammed into her workstation by an unusually large contingent of advertising clients, the air conditioning failed, then the computers, wiping Phoebe's work away in a flash of darkness. The sports car she'd transformed into a white wolf during its race along a coastal road disappeared as the vectorscopes and color wheels dissolved into static. Three tense hours followed, during which the technicians tried to retrieve her work and the clients, pacing in the atrium, swilled coffee. On the telephone in the company kitchen, Phoebe confided her secret hope to Vladimir: that the Harriet would keep her images locked in its dark memory.

"Why?" he'd wanted to know.

Now, inside the cave called Lascaux II, Phoebe thinks she understands. The original Lascaux was closed thirty years ago, and here she is studying, she is assured, a perfect reproduction of ice age art, the walls filled with vibrant images of long-dead animals: black bulls, red deer, yellow horses, falling cows, fanciful unicorns, bison, ibex. But Phoebe finds it impossible to marvel at pigments applied in 1980. The only wonder for her at Lascaux II is the knowledge that there's still a Lascaux I, buried, not dead but unborn, its dark paintings smoldering with life that Phoebe knows burns brightest in the absence of light.

During the third week of her vacation, Phoebe takes a picnic to the banks of the Vézère, under the looming cliff of the Roque Saint-Christophe. The limestone scarp stretches half a mile along the river, with scores of black caves riddling its face and a dark incision running its length, a massive natural ledge cut deep into the cliff. She visited the Roque a week earlier and wandered up its terraces, its hand-cut rock stairways, to poke into its caves. She saw where Neanderthals lived seventy thousand years ago and where Cro-Magnons moved in forty-two thousand years later.

But this afternoon Phoebe comes simply to sit in the cool grass between the river and the cliff, to drink a bottle of wine, feel the sun, listen to the lowing of cows. A thin stream of cars and bicycles winds its way under the cliff as tiny figures ascend the five terraces and snatches of lectures from tour guides drift down to her in a collage of languages.

If she were thirty years old, Vladimir could flatter her into pregnancy, but now she finds herself defensive of her gains: her time, money, and professional status. She pours the black Cahors wine into a jelly-jar glass and savors its sweaty scent. She does wonder about old age, about the possibility of being alone, but is it really worth trading away what she has now? Yet realistically, there's little hope of saving what she has. Without children, Vladimir will eventually leave her.

A cyclist stops on the road, pegs one leg down for support. Phoebe watches him dismount, dig through his saddle pack, pull out a camera, and duck between two strands of barbed wire to walk across the fields. As he turns to focus, Phoebe can see that the cliff is too large to fit into his frame. The next time he turns, he notices Phoebe.

Would she take his photograph?

Of course.

"Here? With the Roque in the background?" He smiles. He's older than she is, with the wiry physique of a runner.

Phoebe lines him up in the extreme left corner of the foreground, dwarfing him beside the megalith. She snaps the shutter, smiles, hands him back the camera.

"Thank you," he says, sizing her up. "Are you English?"

"American," says Phoebe. "And you?"

"Parisian."

"San Francisco," says Phoebe.

"Okay," he says. "My favorite city besides Paris."

Phoebe smiles. She finds the French aren't sure about Americans in general, but San Franciscans somehow are wonderful.

"This is my third trip through the Dordogne," he says. "This is my favorite part of France."

"Me too," says Phoebe.

"Your third trip?"

"No. Sorry. My favorite place in France. This is only my first trip."

She offers him wine, pours it into the second jelly-jar glass she has brought (was she really hoping to meet someone today?), and they stand together, looking up at the Roque. His name is Jacques. He works for Peugeot, but his passion is cycling. He loves this region because of the unique scenery: its sunken valleys, towering cliffs, and startling castles astride every bend of the river. He's less interested in the caves, which are too dark, too cold for him. Surely Phoebe, from foggy San Francisco, understands that he craves the sunlight after Paris, the big oak and chestnut trees, the meadows, the black shine on the rivers. Jacques wonders, is Phoebe is traveling alone?

"Yes."

"That's unusual."

"Perhaps not so much anymore."

And Jacques, is he alone? Yes, yes, he always takes one vacation alone every year. Is he married? Divorced. Children? Yes, he's embarrassed to admit, six. Six? Ridiculous, he knows, but he was young and had two wives. Is he close to his children? Of course. They're wonderful children, the eldest almost thirty years old.

He goes back to his bicycle to fetch a little walnut cake bought from a farm near Périgeux. It's a specialty of the region. He breaks off a piece and hands it to Phoebe.

She tells him about the Harriet and her work, then confides her new idea about animating a scene of ice age cave art: a pair of woolly mammoths, appearing in the video darkness as they might have appeared by firelight in the caves. "But you would never see the artists," she says. "Only their painting, appearing on the walls as if you yourself were putting it there."

Jacques thinks it's a wonderful idea, quite unique.

"If you don't mind my asking," says Phoebe, "are you absolutely happy having had children?" She struggles with the nuance of this question in French as she refills his wineglass.

"Of course I love my children," says Jacques. "But to be completely honest, in a way, they were very hard on both my marriages, and they left me having to work all the time. Only now can I get any time back for myself. To bicycle, to see France."

"Did you want children, or did your wives?"

"With my first wife, we were young, we both wanted to be parents. With my second wife, she was younger than me, and she wanted them. Me, not so much."

"But you agreed to it?"

"Yes. Of course. I did not feel I could deny that to a woman. It is part of the contract of marriage, *n'est pas?*"

The sun slides into their eyes.

"Were you planning to visit the Roque?" Phoebe asks.

"Yes," says Jacques, and she? No, she saw it last week. "Too bad," he says.

Phoebe gives him a wedge of her *cabecou* cheese wrapped in a piece of newspaper, and he gives her a hunk of his walnut cake. They wish each other well.

The first time Vladimir visited Phoebe at work, he skulked into her video house, as sheepish as a corporate spy. She pulled his chair next to hers in the dusk of the Harriet Suite and ran him through her video portfolio, with its clips of unicorns bursting into life and dancing teapots. Vladimir nudged her out of her chair and took up the electronic stylus to draw her a picture of a stick man with a stick penis running toward a stick woman with balloon breasts. Underneath he wrote, "The Lithuanian Chases the Bird in Pursuit of Love."

In the cave of Font de Gaume, Phoebe finds herself getting teary. She's the lone outsider in a tour group of elderly English people, and the tiny woman standing next to her digs through her purse to hand Phoebe a tissue. "It is lovely, isn't it, dearie?" she says as they study the painting of two reindeer engaged in a head-to-head dance.

"For years," says Madame Binet, their tour guide, "this was believed to be a painting of a battle between two reindeer. But now we realize it is actually a picture of their lovemaking." She waves her flashlight over the contours of the animals. "Here you can see how the male is leaning over the female. And here, if you look closely, you can see how he is licking the female's forehead. It is not a fierce scene at all," she says, "but one of the utmost tenderness."

Four days before they were due to leave for France, Vladimir, who had never been camping, impulsively signed up for a kayaking trip down the Kobuk River in central Alaska instead. He looked defiant when he announced the change of plans to Phoebe, who was leaning against the kitchen counter sipping vodka. Vladimir pulled himself up tall, tilting back his head. Phoebe recognized the posture: Vladimir reclaiming his manhood. *Well, shit,* she thought, *go ahead and throw spears for all I care.*

He drove her to the airport for the trip to France and walked her as far as the security gate, where they parted, Phoebe tearfully, then Vladimir too. Phoebe felt depressed during the entire flight and sank into her seat, using three small bottles of airline wine to ease her into a boneless stupor.

The last time she had talked with Vladimir was by phone from the Gare d'Austerlitz, where she was waiting for her train to Bordeaux. She tried to joke. "Maybe we could invent virtual-reality children. You know, ones we could turn on and turn off at will."

Vladimir grunted.

"We'll work it out," she promised. But when they hung up, Phoebe knew they were both wondering, *How?*

Phoebe's tour guide in the Grottes de Gargas is Yves, a French art student from the Sorbonne who is spending the summer working on the ice age paintings of the Pyrenees. Few tourists make it this far south, and Yves, excited at his audience of one, is demonstrating for Phoebe how the paintings were made. He pinches bits of powdered pigments from the little clay bowls at his feet, stuffs them into his mouth, and chews until a blood-red foam seeps from between his lips. Placing his hand on the wall, he leans in and sprays the paint in bursts from his mouth. When he takes his hand away, a perfect stencil appears on the wall. He smiles. "Would you like to try?"

Phoebe chews as Yves watches closely. "You must chew until it's a thin paste," he says. Phoebe smiles, shakes her head: it isn't ready yet. Yves looks sympathetic. "The taste is not too terrible, no?" Phoebe shakes her head again. Actually, she likes the metallic tang of the minerals. When she lays her hand on the cave wall it feels cold, and the spray of paint from her mouth is warm. Her print, when she takes her hand away, looks small, the fingers curved outward.

Yves takes her into the main cavern and runs his light across the ceiling until he finds a print directly overhead. "Here," he whispers. "You can see how badly mutilated this one is." His spotlight hovers over a twenty-thousand-year-old hand, the upper joints of all four fingers clearly missing.

"Jesus," says Phoebe.

"And this one," said Yves, "is missing the upper two thirds of all four fingers."

"Jesus Christ," says Phoebe.

"And here," says Yves, "is one missing three fingers."

"Is it just a few hands?" Phoebe asks. "You know, the same ones over and over again?"

"No," says Yves, "the prints are of hundreds of different hands. And they're not just folding their fingers down. Here you can see where the amputation was made, between the joints. And here the scar is misshapen."

"Why?" asks Phoebe.

"Of course we will never know," says Yves. "But even today there are tribes in New Guinea who amputate the finger joints of girl children, just like this, to express grief when a family member dies."

"And what's that?" asks Phoebe, squinting up into the light.

Yves moves his flashlight back a few inches. "These are the

handprints of children," he says. "And over here" — he flips the light to the opposite wall — "are the hands of very small babies." Phoebe studies the prints, the tiny, perfectly intact fingers stenciled in still-vibrant red and black.

On her last evening in the Dordogne, Phoebe strolls along the banks of the Vézère. The river eddies around the submerged tips of willow branches as caravans of holiday canoes spin inexpertly downstream. Phoebe admires the grace of the landscape, the small motions and unhurried pace. Vladimir would love it, would lie back in the grass on the banks of the river as Phoebe played with his hair and told him her idea for the Harriet. First, how firelight would appear on the mottled brown-and-white limestone of a cave wall, the torch unseen but red flashes from the flames washing through, highlighting the stumps of old stalactites and casting deep shadows into the hollows. Then a fine splatter-pattern of black would emerge and grow into a sinuous line around a natural bulge in the wall. A second line would appear around a second, rounder bulge. A third line would connect the two. Three lines, magic: two mammoths, long trunks curled around each other, tusks interlocked, humped shoulders flowing into shaggy backs.

Phoebe meanders up the winding road to the row of ancient houses built into the base of the cliffs in Les Eyzies-de-Tayac. Honey-colored stones glow in the last sunshine as electric lights burn behind lace curtains. Phoebe listens to family talk spilling out the open windows, watches young girls setting dinner tables, smells the perfume of black truffles and onions. She finds herself envying the clan warmth and affection and begins to plan a new phase to her cave-art animation. The black-and-red splatter-pattern will emerge in the mottled firelight, but as quickly as it appears it will begin to disappear, eroding grain by grain, until only a faint outline of the two mammoths remains, trunks entwined, a suggestion, then nothing.

She walks past the houses to the next terrace and gazes down at the gauzy darkness sifting into the valley. In Cro-Magnon times the caves would be lit with flickering campfires, threads of smoke spinning up to the stars as tigers roared. She would be eating reindeer meat while a Cro-Magnon baby lay curled in her arms. She feels the yearning for it, the need, but also the weight, with her breasts as big as watermelons and the baby hooked up to them. Pounding the marrow out of bison bones, Phoebe wonders, *Where is Vladimir?* Making cave paintings, she's sure, while she stokes the fire and tosses stones to keep hungry bears away.

Nothing has changed. She has always in a way lived without him, since the beginning.

Jimmy Under Water

HE HEARD the ice cracking, the sound traveling up through the soles of his feet as fissures shot out around him and the surface of the lake sagged. Jimmy saw that he was trapped in the center of a web of broken ice, that he was too heavy, that water lay beneath the now obviously transparent surface and was lapping at its underside like a great gray tongue. He was nearly to shore, but that was no help. Two thoughts arose: he was eleven years old and he was about to die. When the ice finally gave way, the cold entered his clothes like fire as he tried to scramble out, arms flailing. But the ice dissolved into rubble, and within moments his joints had locked solid and could no longer keep him afloat. "Help," he croaked to his three friends, who stood on shore and stared. The last thing he saw as he went under was his sled gracefully balanced on the edge of the hole.

. . .

The ice in Antarctica is altogether different from the lake ice in Minnesota, some of it being centuries or perhaps millennia old and as tough as cast iron. Falling through it is impossible. In fact, getting through it at all requires a person to drive a drilling rig on tank treads at a lumbering three kilometers an hour out from the McMurdo Research Station, while emperor penguins tobogganing on their bellies pass easily by.

It's a noisy trip inside the cab of the huge Caterpillar, and Jimmy finds that despite having made the journey many times before, he's still anxious. Simon, his colleague and research partner, uses the GPS to pinpoint their study site from last summer before starting the drill. Its huge corkscrew bit screams as it bites into solid ocean. Jimmy busies himself peeling off his foam rubber–lined exposure suit, wool sweater, wool shirt, thermal undershirt, fleece-lined jeans, thermal underpants, outer socks, and inner socks. He's got the heater inside the Cat cranking at maximum, but even so it's cold, and for a moment, shivering and naked, he stares at his frostbitten feet with the missing toes.

"Jimmy," shouts Simon above the drill, "get dressed."

He dons three layers of long underwear, first a thin white silk, followed by a union-suit thermal, then a furry gray synthetic that makes him look like a yeti, especially with its odd three-fingered mittens. On top of all that goes a Day-Glo purple ski suit. Normally Jimmy wears his own custom-made drysuit, but when he tested it at the station yesterday he noticed a weak seal along one of the seams, so today he wears Simon's suit. It's way too big, as is Simon, but there's really no such thing as a too-big drysuit, and he wrestles the rubber mass of it, fighting the absurdly tight gaskets at wrists and ankles and, worst of all, the hood. It's like trying to be born again, squeezing through the clammy darkness of the neck. Once the hood is on, welded to his head, he's nearly deaf.

"Almost through," shouts Simon over the roar of the drill bit.

"What?" shouts Jimmy.

Simon glances at him, sees the hood, shrugs, then panto-mimes the drill, pointing down at the ice, finger going in circles. They cut this seal-hole yesterday, a four-hour job. Today they're only piercing the last twenty-four hours' skin. Jimmy waddles down the stairs from the cab of the Cat, slipping and falling the last two steps. It doesn't matter; he's as well padded as a polar bear. Simon holds up his thumb, a question. Jimmy flips him a thumb back. He's fine. Frankly, they're maternal toward each other out here, and why not, Jimmy thinks. It's clearly adaptive in this brutal climate. Everyone at the station bonds with a partner, some as broody as old hens. The few who don't seem strange, like caricatures of men, pumped up, over-adrenalized, dangerous even to themselves and to anyone who might have to save them from their notions of independence.

The drill stops. Inside Jimmy's hood all is quiet, only the shush of blood coursing through his veins. He stares at the water swirling in the ice hole, where a few stunned krill ride the eddies. In theory, the drysuit should keep him as separate from this frigid sea beneath the ice as an astronaut is from the vacuum of space. Still, it's been a year since he has done this tricky work, and he remembers to belay himself mentally through each step of the job before committing his body to it.

Simon checks his gauges, shouts, "Three thousand pounds of air." Jimmy nods. They both know it's far more than he'll ever need down there. Long before he can breathe it all he'll be a shivering wreck. Jimmy pulls on his facemask with the regulator attached, so he can't drown even if he loses consciousness, straps his dive computer onto his wrist, crosses one leg, then the other, yanks his fins on, and swings his legs over the edge of the hole, the pressure of the water pinching the loose folds of the drysuit tight against his ankles. Wriggling into the shoulder harness of the scuba tank, he feels Simon attaching the low-pressure hose from the tank and bleeding air into the drysuit. The heat inside it now makes him feel like he is in a self-generated steamroom, Jimmy's sweat, fear, and claustrophobia mixing together.

"I hate drysuits," he says to Simon. Through the regulator it comes out sounding like *Ii-aii-ii-ouos.*

Simon nods, places the video camera in its underwater housing on the edge of the ice hole. He dives too, but on alternate days from Jimmy, because of the extreme toll it takes on their mental and physical reserves.

Jimmy gives Simon a thumbs-up.

"Whoa," says Simon. "Hang on. Your lifeline."

It's early in the season. Behind them, the stone-and-snow cone of Mount Erebus vents its volcanic breath, reminding them that there is land here. A pair of emperor penguins waddles drunkenly north, toward open water. Drawing abreast of the Caterpillar, they stop to stare, heads swinging back and forth as they look first with one eye, then the other, observing the curious actions of Jimmy and Simon on the edge of the ice hole. As an undergraduate, Jimmy thought he might study penguins, but instead he found himself drawn to the chemical mysteries that enable the dwellers of the polar sea, fish and krill, to survive full-time in subzero water. Yet the birds still in-

trigue him, with their ability to tolerate both the frozen sea
and the frigid air.

Flopping onto their stomachs, the penguins paddle away,
leaving rounded trails in the snow punctuated by the apostro-
phes created by their wingtips. It's a fine day for Antarctica, the
sun shining but the wind blowing spindrift as sharp as staples.
The only place it hits skin is on a thin strip of Jimmy's forehead. He turns away. Simon, his face protected by a nuclear-
green balaclava, lumbers over to the Caterpillar, retrieves the
nylon line attached to the front, then ties it to the rescue
buckle on the back of Jimmy's drysuit.

"Okay," he says, patting Jimmy on the shoulder.

Hoisting himself off the edge of the ice, Jimmy slumps into
the water. For a minute he feels the old panic and fumbles with
the buckles on his facemask so Simon won't see.

Despite the burn of cold water, sinking into the Minnesota
lake all those years ago had been strangely comfortable, Jimmy's muscles paralyzed and helpless, his arms and legs, bulky
inside the snowsuit, wrapping around him in a self-embrace
as he pirouetted in slow motion to the bottom, fifteen feet
down. The light under the ice was as lustrous and blue as a
popsicle on that winter day. The only discomforts were the
shock of icewater flooding inside his hood and the thump as
his head hit the bottom, exploding a silt storm that closed out
the light.

For a long time he lay on the bottom, not swimming or
breathing or dying. Long enough for the silt to settle over him.
Long enough for him to see that two of his three friends were
still standing on the high snowbank above, peering through
the slushy ice. The view was disturbing, he down here, his

friends up there, this strange inescapable realm separating them. So he closed his eyes, and in that moment all the muscles in his face went slack and his jaw fell open and the water flooded inside.

Now, beneath the seal-hole, as the cold water on his forehead seems to eat to the bone and a trickle oozes in through the neck valve of his drysuit, Jimmy reassures himself that this is normal. His underlayers will wick it up. Still, anything more than a seep would be disastrous. If he ever really sprang a leak, the suit would fill with water, and not even Simon would have the strength to haul him in. They've discussed that. They'd use the Cat, of course, but it would be a cadaver retrieval, not a rescue.

He hangs just under the seal-hole, reluctant to leave its orifice, watching his exhaust bubbles weave upward, then bump against the underside of the ice. He feels Simon tugging on the tether and reaches behind to tug back. All's well.

Simon is surely noticing that Jimmy's not descending. That's okay. First dive of the season is a fuckless wonder as far as data go. Just get your bearings. Get steady. Later on they'll begin to identify and count the species living under there and map their movements. He presses the bleeder valve on his chest and air streams out of the drysuit and bounces up inside the cage of ice. Jimmy sinks.

Dying all those years ago in the lake was a seamless experience. Jimmy lay on the bottom and the cold settled into him. That was all. It froze him, then froze him some more. He became aware of his heartbeat slowing, the lengthening interval of stillness bracketing each contraction. It seemed the right thing to do under the circumstances, and he remembers thinking, *I am a good boy.*

Now, under the sea ice, Jimmy looks around. Just as planned, Simon parked them over their old study site: the grid they laid out last summer. The yellow nylon line in three-meter squares is still intact in the deeper reaches but plowed to chaos in the shallows by rampaging icebergs. Swimming along the perimeter, he begins to film. Tonight they'll analyze the video and plan Simon's dive tomorrow to re-lay the grid.

The bottom is gray, sandy silt dragged from the land and ground up by the ice, its surface dimpled by millions of clams, buried but for their siphons. Except for the occasional penguin jetting by, or a seal, all under here is still. This is an illusion, Jimmy knows. In reality, a yellow sea spider standing on the bottom is in motion, tiptoeing incrementally from here to there, making, at best, a centimeter an hour. Straddling Grids 7-C and 7-D, a companionable huddle of red sea stars seems frozen to the carcass of a Weddell seal. This is also an illusion. In truth, each star is wrestling and squirming in extremely slow motion, Sumo-style, to the bottom of the pile, hoping to make contact with the carrion, evert its stomach, and begin to digest the flesh. Speed notwithstanding, the aggression is fierce, and those stars that can't elbow in with all or most of their five arms will lose out on what may be the only meal of a fleeting Antarctic summer.

At the bottom of the cold Minnesota lake, heartbeat fading to a shiver, Jimmy left his body. From the outside he looked small, not as he'd felt himself to be. Slowly he began to drift up to where Frankie and Tommy sat on the lake bank, perched on their Radio Flyers, staring into the water.

"I guess he's dead by now," said Frankie.

Already the slush was healing solid.

"Yeah," said Tommy.

Jimmy, this other Jimmy, could see their fear in a kind of black aura. It was not so much fear of death as the fear of what was going to happen to them as a result of it.

Fifteen minutes into his dive under the Antarctic ice, despite swimming hard along the lines of the grid, Jimmy is shaking uncontrollably. He continues to film, knowing it will be ugly but useful. At twenty minutes under he feels Simon tugging at the tether, and he pulls back. Now Jimmy does what he always does with the last moments of a dive: turns off the camera and releases the air from his drysuit as he bumps to the bottom, silt wafting over him. Slowly he turns onto his back to stare up at the ceiling of ice, its underside soft and rounded like the bellies of clouds, only green. To his left is a lone fish, a marbled notothenia, also lying on the seabed. Jimmy checks the thermometer on his dive computer. Minus three tenths of a degree Centigrade. By all the laws of science, that fish should be frozen solid, its cells punctured by crystals of ice, and yet it stares at him, comfortable in this hostile realm. Jimmy wonders: without the glycopeptides this fish carries in its intercellular tissues and blood, how did he survive his icy plunge nineteen years ago?

Fifteen minutes after Jimmy fell through the Minnesota ice, the search-and-rescue team arrived in a truck: two men in wetsuits, a captain, who drove, and eleven-year-old Simon, sitting up front. The team went to work, laying out the hoses, starting the generator on the truck, and firing up the compressor to feed air through the hookah as Simon stood on the edge of the lake beside Frankie and Tommy, peering in. Ordering the boys uphill, the divers inched cautiously, feet first, into the water. Jimmy could see that they were frightened. Both for him, the Jimmy under water, and for themselves, who had to find him.

"Grab him," shouted Simon into the water.

"They can't hear you," said Tommy.

The flashing lights of an ambulance bounced off the snow-banks as paramedics unloaded a gurney and laid towels and blankets on top of it. One diver's head broke through the surface, his face purple from the cold as he pulled the regulator from his mouth, hands twitching, breath steaming. "Can't find him," he sputtered.

"Try to the left," shouted the captain.

The diver nodded, bit down again on the regulator.

"He's under the sled," shouted Simon as the diver sank, his bubbles stirring the slush. "I could find him," he said, almost hopping with frustration.

"Shit, Simon," whispered Frankie, pulling him away. "Leave them alone."

Some part of Frankie, something around his ears, was now tremblingly green, like fireflies. It was fascinating how Jimmy knew that Frankie was ready and even excited to embark on the adventure of having a dead friend.

Alone on his back at the bottom of the Antarctic sea, Jimmy collects his thoughts, closes his eyes. Okay. He's ready. Carefully he stops breathing and pulls off his mask and regulator. He feels the cold against his face in an instant, agonizing head-ache, and his jaw clenches from the pain. He forces himself to relax until his mouth falls open and the water enters, searing his teeth, his tongue. Opening his eyes, he groans, bubbles spiraling up to the ice roof as his body seizes from the pain. He allows himself a moment of self-pity before reminding himself why he must do this. Somewhere in this realm where living things slow to an almost complete stop without actually ceasing, where starfish remain motionless for up to a year at a time, where the lives of fish span decades or perhaps centuries, life begins to approximate infinity. This is the real subject of Jimmy's research.

Time also passed slowly nineteen years ago. Critical time for Jimmy under water. Thirty minutes. Thirty-two. The paramedics moved to the edge of the ice, peering in. The captain fielded radio calls to the police as the divers searched ever more frantically through the silt, billows of it roiling to the surface and staining the slush black.

At last a diver burst up, his regulator falling from his mouth. "Got him," he shouted.

The other diver surfaced too. Head still bowed into the water, he clawed his way to shore, hauling something that came partially out of the water: a shoulder, then an arm, followed by Jimmy's head, the neck so limp it looked broken, the face streaky, dull blue. Water poured out of him as the paramedics took him from the divers and raced up the hill.

Now the answer that Jimmy has waited for for so long lies just beyond the cusp of consciousness. He can feel its presence, not embodied, not something you could shake hands with, but something. Simon is tugging on the tether. Ignore it. Tug. Twenty-five minutes, time to leave. Forget about it. But how can he? Simon, the bastard. Too late. The answer is coming out of Jimmy as if on a fishhook and line. He snaps his teeth together, trying to hold it inside.

Wrenching the mask down onto his face, Jimmy punches the purge valve, and water gushes out, followed by air. Simon is hauling him now, dragging him up. Hell. He can swim. But when he tries, his legs spasm uncontrollably. Dragged backward by the buckle, bleeding air into his drysuit for buoyancy, Jimmy ascends until he collides with the ice. That's unpleasant. Simon is hauling him in like a spent fish, his head and shoulders grinding against the ceiling. He tries to reorient himself in order to fend off the ice with his arms and in the process finds his legs beginning to kick, enough to keep him from bumping against the roof. By the time he gets to the seal-hole he has managed to turn himself around and self-locomote.

At the surface, water sluicing off his mask, he can see Simon yelling, but he can't hear what. Fumbling to unsnap the scuba tank, he wiggles out of the harness and holds it at the surface for Simon to grab. But Simon's still shouting, his eyes in the holes of the balaclava sparking with fear. Jimmy makes a circle with his thumb and forefinger and holds it up, the universal divers' sign for "I'm all right." Only partially reassured, Simon nods and reaches for the tank. Jimmy remembers the look. When the siren started and the ambulance surged forward, skidding and bouncing against the snow beside the lake, Jimmy watched Simon's doubting face receding behind him on the road.

Aboard the Caterpillar, Jimmy is shaking so hard with cold that twice he lurches out of his seat. Simon screeches through the gears, shouting the whole way. "What the hell happened down there?"

"Got really cold," Jimmy says, teeth chattering.

"Well, why didn't you come up sooner?"

"Didn't realize."

"Christ almighty. You should've signaled me. I would've hauled you in."

"You did."

"I know I did."

"Thanks," says Jimmy. "Didn't know I needed help."

"You didn't know?" says Simon. "You're swimming and swimming and suddenly you can't swim and you don't know you need help?"

Jimmy reaches to the dashboard to turn up the heat, but his arms are jerking so much he can't land his fingers on the lever. "Wasn't swimming," he says.

"You weren't swimming?"

Suddenly he's absolutely, completely drained. It's always this way after ice diving: not a morsel of energy at the end of it. He gives up on the lever.

Simon adjusts the heat for him. "What were you doing?"

Jimmy has never told Simon about what he does at the end of each dive. "Lying on the bottom," he says.

"Lying on the fucking bottom? Doing what?" But Simon doesn't wait for an answer that neither of them wants to hear. "Well, take a shower when you get back," he says. "Get warm."

Jimmy nods. It's what they always do after ice diving: stand under the hot water until their extremities burn with returning life.

Aboard the ambulance, Jimmy watched the paramedics tend his lifeless body, one cutting the wet clothing away, hands and arms expertly weaving in and around the ministrations of the other, who rhythmically administered CPR. On the third round of heart massage, Jimmy reentered his body, slipping in through the nose and riding the breath of life down into his lungs, where he once again became part of the body that for the last thirty-eight minutes had been unconscious, then dead, now unconscious again.

They worked on his core temperature for four hours in the emergency room before they got it close to normal. The first thing Jimmy remembered when he awoke was seeing through his eyes again: the strange sight of his parents crying and rubbing his hands as Simon waited behind them.

"Hi," said Jimmy.

"Who's that?" asked a doctor, pointing to Jimmy's mother.

"Mom," whispered Jimmy.

"What's your name?" said the doctor.

"Jimmy."

"How old are you?"

"Eleven."

"Amazing," said the doctor.

"What's the password?" said Simon, stepping closer.

Jimmy paused and smiled. "I'm not gonna say that here."

Now he's alone, eating a huge steak ("6 cms Thick," the mess blackboard states), mounds of french fries, and cole slaw as well as a second plate heaped with spaghetti and meatballs. Jimmy alternates monstrous bites with slugs of boiling hot coffee. It's always like this after a dive: eat and eat and still shiver. He has already showered and put on damn near every piece of clothing he owns. Normally Simon would be eating with him.

Jimmy finds him in the ice lab, tending their captives, the Antarctic limpets and the specimens of *Serolis polita,* including a pregnant one bursting with pink eggs, some krill, and a lone, prized icefish. Simon nets a krill, but when he realizes that Jimmy is there, he turns away. Jimmy watches the krill contract violently as Simon plucks her from the net and drops her onto a petri dish, where the beating of her heart inside her translucent body is blurred by speed.

Go in peace is what Jimmy thinks whenever he sacrifices some living thing. Or sometimes, simply, *Sorry.*

Simon grunts, shrugs, and Jimmy realizes he must have said it aloud.

Holding the krill with a forceps, Simon expertly inserts a hypodermic into her heart to extract her blood. It's as clear as dew. No oxyhemoglobin here, just hemocytes. Jimmy watches as her swimming legs beat. It's what she has always done, swim and swim from the moment of her birth. She dies from the inside out, her clear tissues clouding up as her legs fall still.

The next morning Simon is polite but distant, refusing to ask Jimmy for help. In his drysuit, bedecked with the toolkit, hammer, stakes, and a coil of yellow nylon line, he looks like some oversized cartoon character: good or evil, Jimmy's not sure which. Simon is the only diver Jimmy knows who can walk with all his ice-diving gear on. Everyone else sits on the edge of the hole and falls over. But Simon makes an elegant, nearly splashless step-entry and the water closes over him.

Jimmy notes the time of Simon's entry in the log before returning to the Cat to collect Simon's clothes from the floor and fold them roughly in a heap on the warm crankcase. At the edge of the seal-hole he retrieves the nylon tether. It's overcast today. A snow as thin as dandruff is falling, although it's questionable whether it's really falling or simply being blown off the ground, swirled around, and dropped again. Even with his exposure suit and polar boots Jimmy can feel the cold biting into his feet and knees. He watches a pair of emperor penguins approach, beaks bobbing as they circle the Cat once, then flop onto their stomachs and toboggan over to where Jimmy sits with the rescue line draped across his lap.

"Hello," he says.

In one motion they flip from the horizontal to the vertical. Standing now, they wait alongside him, peering down into the water. He checks his watch.

Five minutes. He gives three tugs.

No answer. He tugs, three times, evenly spaced. A penguin bends over and pecks at the line snaking across the ground. "Simon," he says. Three more tugs, and again. Okay, shit. That's enough. Jimmy stands, braces himself, and begins to haul. Nothing. He tries again. No good. He can't move the line. It's like trying to tow an iceberg. He can feel the panic but pushes it away and heaves again until he believes he can actually see the line stretching. Still nothing. He runs for the cab of the Cat.

The engine is still running, but the clutch is stubborn. He works the gearshift, trying to coax it into reverse, eventually ramming it into gear and inching backward. The line slowly tightens until a sound like a rifle report pings through the chassis. He can't believe what he's seeing. The line is broken. One half recoils toward him. The other slithers over the edge and down the seal-hole.

The base director, Howard, will not allow Jimmy to dive for Simon, and although he can't stop Jimmy from suiting up, he won't give him any air. Instead he sends two rescue divers in, a pair of amphipod guys from UC. It's everyone's nightmare, and Jimmy can see it on their faces. It could have been one of them. Jimmy paces, working up a sweat inside the drysuit. Howard is calm. He doesn't seem to understand the urgency.

"It's been forty-two minutes," says Jimmy.

"Put on your balaclava," says Howard.

"You know he can be revived."

"I know," says Howard. "Put on your balaclava."

Jimmy pushes back his hood, pulls down the balaclava, realizing as he looks through the eyeholes that it's not his but Simon's.

A diver rises to the surface, lifts his mask and regulator. "Found him."

Howard nods. "Can we bring him in?"

"We're ready."

They use a polar tow truck, winching him up ridiculously slowly, the deliberate and lugubrious pace of everything in the Antarctic. Jimmy finds himself hating it all: the ice, the cold, the slow-motion burgling of life.

As kids, Simon always envied Jimmy's accident scars. The missing toes. Frostbite burns. It was manly stuff. Now Jimmy studies the indentations on Simon's lips where he was intubated with the respirator and examines the holes in his arms and on the back of his hands where they inserted blood and gas monitor lines, saline, and who knows what else. There's still a piece of surgical tape on Simon's nose, which Jimmy peels off. He notices the crescent-shaped scar on the left knee and has to think for a moment before remembering the time Simon fell off his bike on Lakeville Street after Jimmy tossed a cherry bomb at him.

For a while everyone explains things to him. The base doctor tells him why children do better in cold-water submersion than adults. The rescue divers describe how they found Simon wedged behind a grounded iceberg in only four meters of water and how they had to dig away the bottom to get him free. Howard, alone with Jimmy in the bunkhouse, talks about the drysuit. It was frayed along the upper back, with a small tear in the right shoulder that filled with water. Any idea how that could have happened? Jimmy shakes his head. But he suspects it must have happened when he was dragged along the ceiling of ice the day before. And Howard wonders, didn't Simon signal his distress? Didn't he tug on the line? Jimmy feels incredibly dull-witted. He can't actually think. He can only remember folding Simon's clothes.

At three o'clock that night, or morning, or whatever it is in this relentlessly bright realm of the polar summer, Jimmy watches the weak beam of the sun circle the horizon through a haze of snow. Already the seal-hole is plugged with new ice. He sits beside it, cold, waiting, while far off to the north a line of penguins glides toward open water. Lucky birds, he thinks, feathers fitting as tightly as scales, filoplumes to trap warm air, subcutaneous pads of fat. Jimmy shivers, then finds himself jumping up, waving his arms. But his movements are those of a frozen man, a snowman, and when he shouts, a peculiar moan rushes away from him on the wind, the wrong way with respect to the penguins. Even so, the last bird in line glances over, stops, swivels on its wings, then paddles toward him. Jimmy wonders, why is this bird doing this? Suddenly, gratefully, he asks himself why it trusts him.

The Daguerreotype

I HAVE THE DEATH PORTRAIT of my great-grandmother's baby who died from the measles in 1871. My great-grandmother's name was Florence Belva Parnell, and she was only nineteen years old when her firstborn died. In the daguerreotype, the infant is propped upright in a white christening gown, which offers no clue to its gender. Dried blood is smudged under its nose, and five fresh measles welts mark its forehead. Wearing mourning taffeta and looking very young, my great-grandmother cradles the back of her baby's head in one hand. She slumps her own head into her other hand. She doesn't look at the camera, but the baby does. Straight at it, eyes partly open, the left lid a little heavier than the right. Its expression reminds me of my childhood doll, who had too many cups of sugar water spilled on her during tea parties, so that when I laid her down to sleep one eye stuck open, and when I sat her up to feed her both eyes stuck closed.

I found the daguerreotype when I was ten years old and looking for the sex manual I had seen under my father's sweaters on the top shelf in his closet. I dragged a chair up from the kitchen and stretched on tiptoes until my arches cramped, remembering the drawings of penises and vaginas and how amazingly they fit together. Having seen these pictures once was not enough. I needed to confirm my memories: Were such things possible? Were they likely? I worked through the closet by feel, sweeping my hand under my father's smooth merino cardigan, between two cotton crewnecks and an oiled wool Aran Isles sweater stiff with age. Instead I found the daguerreotype inside a paper wrapping that said *Britt's Daguerreotype Studio, San Francisco.*

At the time I thought that the dark-haired woman looked tired and that she was holding her child's head because the baby would not behave for the camera. I had no idea the infant was dead. But then again, I thought my father was hiding the sex manual from my mother.

Nine years later, when I was writing a term paper on the development of photography for an art history class, I asked my mother if I could see the daguerreotype.

"That old thing?" she said, digging through my father's desk in search of it.

"Who are they?" I asked.

"That was your father's grandmother."

"What was her name?"

"She was a Parnell," said my mother.

"What was her first name?"

"Florence, I believe."

"Was I named for her?"

"I guess your father was thinking of something like that. I just liked the name." She went back to her painting, a watercolor of the light as it dripped through a maidenhair fern in the window.

"Doesn't sunlight kill ferns?" I asked.

"Yes," said my mother. "But isn't it beautiful?" She continued to twitch her brush across the paper until little pinpoints of green bled into the wash of water, spreading beyond the boundaries of her brush. Watercolor is the only paint that continues to grow after you put it to paper. I never could understand how my mother controlled it.

"And is this baby Dad's father or mother?" I asked.

"Neither," said my mother. "That was a child who died."

"When did it die?"

"It's dead right there." She pointed with the long handle of the watercolor brush.

"It's dead here?" I pulled the picture close.

"That's a death portrait," said my mother, as matter-of-fact about death as about the mysteries of watercolor.

"Is it a boy or a girl?" I asked.

"No one remembers."

After that I switched the subject of my term paper to nineteenth-century death photography. Evidently the Victorians took pictures of their dead as readily as of the living, and in many cases the death portrait was the only picture of a person, particularly of a child, that ever existed. Many photographers took care to pose the corpses in lifelike ways, sitting them in chairs with their eyes closed and hands crossed in their laps, as if thinking pleasant thoughts while awaiting Sunday visitors, or reclining on settees, heads tilted to the side, perhaps listening to poetry in the next room.

I sent my mother the finished report with the professor's "B+, nice work, interesting subject" on it, and my mother sent me back one of her characteristic handwritten notes:

> Dear Florence,
>   Your typing is shaping up nicely. I noticed there weren't too many whiteouts.
>
> Love,
> Mom
>
> P.S. I've enclosed a snapshot of my newest watercolor: the light from a forest fire reflected on a calypso orchid.

When I was twenty-five years old, a secretary, and pregnant by the married man who employed me and whom I thought I loved, I found myself preparing for the ordeal of my first abortion. I'd kept the daguerreotype with me since the writing of the term paper and now took it out of the coat closet where I kept my photo albums. My great-grandmother's fingers were curled around the baby's ear and pressed into its downy hair as if she had been stroking it in the private moments while the photographer prepared the shot. She didn't appear the least appalled that this was the corpse of her baby, only sad. Boneless from grief, I thought.

When I was thirty years old, my father chose to leave my mother to live alone, largely unemployed, in the scrub pines on the western slope of the Sierra Nevada. "I'm sick of marriage," he told me when I asked him why. "If I want to live on cans of stew and smoke in the house and wear dirty clothes, by god, I'm going to." I stopped trying to clean up around his place after that and spent my visits just talking with him. I was still interested in Florence Belva Parnell and what he knew of her.

"Your grandfather remembered a little," he said one night as we sat in the old kitchen chairs that he had scrounged from some flea market and set up behind his cabin. The only saving grace to his ramshackle property, as far as I could tell, was the stars. They lived in abundance out there, crowding the sky with light. He'd taught me the constellations many years before, but here the cosmos seemed larger and more brilliant, and for the first time I really understood that the sky my father loved glittered with stars that had been extinct for eons, that existed only as traveling light.

"When Florence was sixteen, she went west with her parents on a wagon train from Iowa," he said. "They were headed out on the Overland Trail for Oregon, but her parents died of cholera somewhere in Nebraska. Florence hooked up with a widower named Birthright Parnell on the same wagon train, only he took the south fork in Wyoming and went to California. They got married in San Francisco, ran a saloon there, and raised Birthright's son from his previous marriage, along with his two nephews, whom he'd taken on after his brother drowned during the crossing of the Platte River. Birthright, I guess, had a thing for orphans. When Florence was thirty-seven, she gave birth to the only one of her twelve children who survived past the age of seven. That was my father, Lucky Parnell."

"And?"

But my father told me that it was time to stop talking because the Perseids were running. He clamped his mouth shut and lifted his head to the night. When he was younger, my father took time-lapse photographs of meteor showers that made the silver stars look like stalactites dripping from the sky. Both my parents knew the secret of making small pictures grow larger.

I let my head drop back and allowed my focus to blur, knowing that to see shooting stars you have to set your eyes free.

"The Perseids were named because they appear to shoot like arrows from the constellation Perseus, the Archer," my father had told me when I first watched the showers from the dark hills on the far side of the Golden Gate Bridge.

"Who was Perseus?"

"Perseus was the son of Zeus who slew Medusa, then carried her head with him, flashing it at his enemies and turning them into stone. He rescued the beautiful Andromeda from Cetus by using the power of the dead Medusa's head."

"How long did this head last?"

"Forever," he said. "You see, Perseus is still in the sky. Every night he plays out his fate, again and again. And every August he shoots his quiver of arrows through the sky for us to see."

It took a few moments of relaxation in the cold air of my father's mountain before I saw it. But within half an hour the arrows were racing furiously through the sky, bouncing off the edges of my sight, scoring a few direct hits.

"It's a good year," said my father, resting his head on the back of the chair. "The Delta Aquarid meteors are running now too."

I listened to his words and let my eyes drift off to a point of such distant focus that they came almost full circle, to the point of closest focus.

"I wish we had a name for it," I said.

"For what?" he said, his eyes still on the sky.

"Florence's dead baby."

"No use," he said. "It's lost."

"Maybe we should make up a name."

"It had a real name once, and you can't change that."

But secretly I called it Independence.

When I was thirty-seven and pregnant for the third time, I decided to have the baby, even though I wasn't married and couldn't hope to interest the father (another boss, also married) in parenthood. I knew my future with men was likely to be as unhappy as my past, yet felt certain that a child would accept my love. My mother was painting in the front parlor of the old Victorian she'd bought after my father died when I told her the news.

To my surprise, she was delighted, and told me that motherhood was far better than wifehood and I'd chosen the right half of the equation to balance my budget on. Then she cleaned her brushes and wiped them dry.

A week later I received a package from her in the mail. She had bought an antique picture frame with leather edging and hand-worked wood carving.

> Dear Florence,
>
> You can put the baby's picture in here when it's born. I am very happy about your news.
>
> Love,
Mom
>
> P.S. I won first place in the Art Fair for my painting of the light shining through Mrs. Rosen's window at night.

It was a beautiful frame, and as I had no baby picture yet, I decided to put the daguerreotype in it. I tucked it away in

my underwear drawer, intending someday to replace the daguerreotype with my child's picture, but I never did.

Before she was born I knew that my baby would be a girl, and I
decided to name her Florence Independence Parnell. "For my
great-grandmother," I told my mother. "Not for me."

But I called her Indy from the start. Holding her in my lap
with one hand on her chest, feeling her heart beat through her
eggshell ribs, I'd look down at her face, studying the tiny blue
veins, memorizing them for the day when her skin would grow
thicker. She'd smile with eyes so new that I couldn't tell if they
were really focused on me or on something farther away.

As Indy grew, she learned the secrets of watercolor from her
grandmother. We visited Petaluma on Sundays and sat in the
big sunny front parlor of the Victorian, my mother and Indy
with their easels and brushes. Together they painted the stems
of cut rununculus in a vase of water, or the slats of light falling through the wooden blinds onto the oriental rug. Indy
twitched her brush across the wet paper, the color starting
small and growing outward.

When she was eleven, Indy questioned me about her background. She was reading *Little Women* that summer, feeling
the deficit of both siblings and a father and questioning me
at length about her history. I'd already explained (not quite
truthfully) why I had never married her father and how he had
died before she turned two. I told her she came from a long
line of single-child families: me, my father, his father. Together
we looked through the old photo albums, laughing at the
snapshots of her infancy. The evidence of her love of peas (she
would collect them from her plate and paste them on her

head), her first day at the beach (crawling after seagulls to offer them cookies), her rides on the back of the polka-dotted rocking horse that my father had built for me, smiling with glee and gripping the handles of the horse's ears.

"I always thought I was flying on that rocking horse," she told me. "We went to Persia and sometimes to Egypt. Did you fly on him too?"

"No, I think I just enjoyed rocking in place."

I hugged her, feeling her curiosity bursting through her bones, knowing that someday it would speed her away from me.

"I have a pretty good idea of how people do it," she said that summer, regarding sex. "But I'm not sure about all the details."

I thought back to my father's manual, the line drawings of body parts. Then told her the truth.

"Is it *fun?*" she asked, skeptical.

I offered my advice. "It's best for love or babies." But she looked so hopeful that I conceded, "Indy, sex may take you places I've never been."

In the aftermath of my mother's death, when Indy was seventeen, I showed her the daguerreotype. We packed up the contents of the old Victorian, put it on the market, and held an estate sale to auction off my mother's belongings. We kept only her paintings, her photo albums, and her letters.

"I've already seen this picture," Indy said. "I found it in your drawer."

I laughed, wondering how I could have failed to know. "This is your great-great-grandmother," I said.

"Who's the baby?"

"That's a baby who died."

"When did it die?"

"This is its death portrait," I said. "In those days people took pictures of the dead as remembrances."

"Really?" said Indy, taking the picture out of my hand. "Why was that?"

"Because the pictures consoled them," I said.

When she was twenty-two, Indy joined the Peace Corps. I had imagined that after four years away at college, she might come back to me for the summer before medical school, and I had repainted her room, bought her a new comforter in midnight blue with flecks like stars on it, and planned trips to the Chabot Observatory, to the redwoods, to Big Sur.

"I'm going to Ghana," she called to tell me.

"Ghana?" I said.

"Isn't it great?"

"What about NYU?" I asked.

"They say I can go as soon as I get back."

"When will that be?"

"In two years," she said proudly.

During the weeks before she left we talked on the phone often. Indy told me about Ghana and the village near Banda Nkwanta in the hills above the Black Volta where she would live. In the local medical clinic she would treat schistosomiasis, sleeping sickness, and malaria. "But I'm going to learn too," she said, "to study the herbal medicines of the region."

I thought of Africa, so far away that we would never share the same daylight, and of Florence Belva Parnell leaving her dead parents in long-forgotten graves on the Nebraska plains. I decided to give Indy one of my father's photographs of the Perseid meteor shower to take with her, as well as the last painting my mother ever made, of the light inside a honey-comb.

"What about you?" she asked. "I want to take something of yours."

I went through all my belongings: the antique gold wedding bands I'd once collected, the Depression glass, the old books and postcards of places I'd never been. In the end I looked in the yellow pages for a professional photographer. San Francisco had hundreds. When I saw a listing for Britt's Photography, I thought it couldn't be possible, yet two days later I found a gray-haired man behind the camera in the old storefront south of Market.

"I want a photograph to give to my daughter to take with her to the Peace Corps," I told him.

"Something special, then," he said.

I nodded. "How long has Britt's been here?"

"Since 1869."

"My great-grandmother had a photograph taken here in 1871."

"Really?" He smiled in amazement. "My great-grandfather probably took it."

"Really?"

"But it wouldn't have been here exactly," he said. "The old studio burned down in the 1906 earthquake."

"I see."

"What kind of portrait would you like?" he asked.

"My daughter would probably like something glamorous. But I'm not sure that's possible."

"What would *you* like?"

I thought for a moment. "I'd like a picture where it looks like I'm watching the stars, or a meteor shower."

A week after the session he sent me pages of contact prints with instructions to circle the one I wanted. There were pictures with my head tilted up to the right and down to the left, and with my eyes looking over the shoulder. I chose the photograph where my head rests in one hand and a bar of light, like in the old movies, illuminates my eyes.

In an antiques store in Petaluma I found a pair of old velvet-and-gilt picture frames and put the prints of my photographs in each of them. I kept one for myself, then wrapped the other in tissue paper that said *Britt's Photography* and gave it to Indy to take with her.

Falling Umbrella

He's driving dutifully in the slow lane, but even so the cars around him are as aggressive as wild dogs, running up to his rear, tripping him in the front, closing along his flanks. He has often thought of this of late, how here on the roads the last of the predator/prey relationship plays itself out in human life. He's old, in fact extremely old, and knows he's something of a lame buffalo limping along the edges of the herd, ready to be weeded out, if not by canids, then by the ceaseless stampede of his own kind.

It's raining as he drives north onto the Golden Gate Bridge. Wind from the Pacific slams his car toward the curb, and his windshield wipers can barely keep up, smearing water and taillights across the glass. Peering for the cat's-eyes dividing the lanes, his eyes darting left and right, he notices the umbrella. The only one on the bridge. A red umbrella with a woman beneath it. A car swerves in front of him and he stomps on the brakes, but his Buick slues sideways toward the curb shielding the edge of the pedestrian walkway. He hears the sounds of airbags detonating around him as BMWs and Lexuses bounce into each other. Because his car is old and has no airbag, he's able to see the woman hop suddenly onto the rail and the umbrella pitch out as a gust of wind lifts it, tilts it. A red flower taking a bow. Then the wind snaps the spokes inside out and the blossom is transformed into a mangle of stainless steel and shredded nylon.

She falls.

That night he sleeps badly and awakens before dawn to rummage around in the kitchen by the light of the open refrigerator door. The chain reaction on the bridge finally ended with an SUV rear-ending his Buick. He jerry-rigs an icepack out of a plastic bag from the grocery store to nurse his broken nose with. The icebag is awkward and doesn't really alleviate the pain, but he doesn't know what else to do. His wife was good at these things, not him. The doctors gave him Tylenol with codeine at the hospital, and a prescription for more, but he didn't fill it. Doesn't like drugs.

He picks up the chalk and begins to doodle on the blackboard above the kitchen counter. What are the odds? It's a simple enough question. Every weekday for, what, fifty-six years he has driven across the bridge. Never before seen anyone jump. How many in total have jumped in those years? He can only speculate at this point. Say 275. That's one on average every 74.3 days. But averages don't calculate the odds that he himself will intersect the exact time and place that a woman decides to go over.

He has grown old. Perhaps his math skills have diminished.

Ever since his wife died, he has found himself questioning the numbers.

Was it coincidence that he was there at exactly that moment? Even more troubling (the part that really upsets any hope of a numerical solution) is the strange reality of the umbrella. He can't find any way to account for why a woman who planned to die in the wet grip of the ocean two hundred feet below would carry an umbrella with her in the rain.

He returns to the problem of her death again and again. In his office, consulting absentmindedly with undergraduates, doodling on the blackboard, trying various proofs by contradiction (the method of infinite descent), he keeps asking, *Why did she jump just then?* Did it have anything to do with his trying to hit the brakes, only missing and slamming the accelerator instead? When the police first speculated on this theory, he was shocked. But now, because frankly, he can't remember exactly what happened, he has allowed himself to discard that notion, although it returns to him at night in his dreams.

He keeps the tiny article tucked into the corner of the blotter on his desk. It's essentially the same newspaper story that runs after every jump or fall from the bridge, addressing the need for safety screens on the pedestrian walkway. In the end, the coroner ruled the death of the woman a suicide. Yet there was no note, and she didn't seem to have any friends to comment on her state of mind. Her family back in the Philippines was mystified. She was only twenty-five years old.

Eight days later he drives himself across the bridge for the first time since the accident. All week he has crossed on the bus, but the view is different from up there. Today he can see what he saw on that rainy evening, albeit going in the opposite direction, and on this sunny weekend morning the pedestrian walkway is crowded with sightseers. He'd like to slow down and examine it all more closely, but he's fearful of the bridge.

Still, his mind reenacts it. The rain. The wind. The step up, the red umbrella becoming a broken parachute. All just as he saw it but then more, elements he can only imagine, yet so vividly that they've almost become memory: the woman swinging slowly downward, light and relaxed. Her eyes closed. The sad but inevitable end to all things that flower. It's an image as beautiful as a perfect piece of geometry, the flawless arc of a sinusoidal oscillation.

His daughter meets him at the Imperial Tea House in Chinatown and touches his cheek lightly.

"Your nose," she says.

"It's better now."

"Why didn't you tell me?"

She consults with the woman behind the counter before ordering Dragon Whiskers green tea for him. He's not sure why. For his kidneys, she says, the organ of fear. He doesn't believe such superstition and at any rate tends to phase out discussions of his health, or anyone's health, for that matter. It was one of the last arguments he had with his wife. She was hurt, he knew, by his lack of involvement in her illness, and one day she became very angry. She could no longer shout, so she wheezed: hissing, whistling accusations. What good was he? What good was a mate if he didn't take care of you when you were ill?

He wished he knew how to help, wished above all he knew how to cure her. But he couldn't in fact face any of it: her growing debilitation, her bewilderment, the bodily corruptions of pain, incontinence, suffocation. His wife's illness was confused and murky and utterly without quantification. Being in its presence was like stepping back into the Dark Ages, and it had frightened him more than anything to learn how inexact medical science was, how there was no correct course of treatment for his wife, only a series of options. In the end she had chosen solely by intuition.

His daughter pours the tea for him.

"Are you sleeping well?" she asks.

"Yes," he lies.

She looks like him, or so he is often told. She certainly doesn't look like his wife. His daughter is also thin, even gawky, and her hair is cropped close, showing the contours of the skull. It's a handsome head, he must admit.

"Carla is fine," she says to him, because he hasn't asked.

"Oh," he says. "That's good."

"She's going to Singapore."

"Forever?"

He trusts that isn't a hopeful note he heard in his voice.

"No, Dad. Not forever. For nine months. On a Fulbright."

"Ah."

His daughter knows (he suspects) that he thinks the problem is solely Carla. His daughter, of course, doesn't think anything is wrong.

"I was hoping to go with her," she says.

"What about your work?"

She has taken his realm, mathematics, and embraced one of its corrupt cousins, economics. If theoretical mathematics is the pure and perhaps divine spirit of the universe, then economics is the whore, working only for money and the salacious desires of its clients. He believes he once told her this, long ago, back in her college days. If anything, it seemed to attract her more to the field.

Her friend Carla is a further mystery to him. Petite, pretty, with pale brown hair and big blue eyes, she is in some ways reminiscent of his wife when she was young.

"I could take a sabbatical," his daughter says. "Work on a book."

"What book?" His voice is sharp.

She pours him some more tea.

"A book I'm thinking of writing. On the history of mathematics."

He feels a sudden pain in his throat.

She hands him a napkin to cough into. Somehow, his daughter seems able to predict all of his reactions, whereas he feels off-balance with her, unable to foresee anything.

"I thought I might consult with you. You know. Tap into some of your own research." She offers him this, along with a cough drop, on the table between them.

He reaches into his jacket, removes the mechanical pencil from his pocket protector and a small notepad. He begins to doodle, drawing a number plane, labeling the real axis and the imaginary axis. "I don't know," he says, his throat still tight.

"Dad," she says, taking back the cough drop and unwrapping it for him. "It could be a collaboration."

He thinks of the stacks of typewritten pages in boxes in the attic, his own unfinished book. Was anything salvageable in them?

"Are you interested?"

He shrugs. He knows it's ungenerous and unfatherly of him to fear his daughter's success, but he can't help it.

Later that afternoon he finds the young Filipina's apartment in the Tenderloin. The building manager is as dirty as the neighborhood, her sweatshirt and sweatpants covered with stains and her bouffant hair bedecked with what looks like small pieces of litter.

She eyes the old man suspiciously.

"It's four stories up," she says.

"That's okay. I'm slow, but I'll make it."

"No, I mean I can't let you up alone," she says.

"All right."

"I ought to go with you." She grunts, and then hands him the key. "But if you try to make off with anything, I suppose it won't be hard to catch you." She laughs.

"Tell me," he asks. "What did she do for a living?"

The manager blinks, perhaps in disbelief. "I thought you said you were representing the family."

He touches the bruised bridge of his nose, which gains him a moment. "They don't know what she did," he says.

"Well. What they all do around here, I guess."

He's not sure what this means.

"You know. Tricks."

He realizes he's old and out of touch. Even so, he's surprised, and then, suddenly, relieved. As if a bath of forgiveness were washing over him. Of course. If she was a prostitute, of course she'd want to kill herself.

"I see."

He debates about walking up the four flights. But he knows the manager still doubts his ability to make the ascent, so he goes.

The stairwell is littered with food and condom wrappers and used hypodermics. He leans heavily on the railing, stopping at each landing. Many years ago, decades ago, his long legs carried him across the Marin Headlands and down to Rodeo Beach every day. They didn't call it jogging then. It was called long-distance running.

A woman passes him. She is small and dark, her legs bare to the hem of a very short skirt. Despite her platform shoes she rattles down the stairway at a rapid clip, like a cloven-footed animal. He notices her breasts, pushed up and out by a tight shirt and bra. Is this what the Filipina looked like? He saw little more of her than a blur in a raincoat.

Her apartment is tiny and nearly empty. There's a single un-made bed and a bureau, the drawers open, unfolded clothes spilling out. An ashtray on top is filled with cigarette butts, and a photograph, unframed, lies covered with ash. He shakes it clean. A family, most likely. A large Filipino family. He tries to imagine which girl or woman in the picture was the occu-pant of this room, but really there's no way to tell. He puts it down. A crucifix with a gilded Christ graces the dirty, other-wise empty walls, and a porcelain statue of Mary sits on the windowsill, her face downcast and gray with grime. Two high-heeled sandals lie on their sides under the window. He bends over slowly, picks one up.

So small.

He drops it.

There's nothing here. Nothing concrete. Just the circum-stantial clues of a meaningless life. Perhaps a tortured life. He would like to assuage his guilt with the thought, but cannot. What does he really know of her, this Filipina? Nothing.

He turns to leave her room. In the corner next to the door leans an umbrella. A green umbrella. He reaches out to see if it's real. The handle is plastic, molded to look like bamboo. He feels his heart accelerate.

"Hey," says a woman in the doorway.

He flinches.

"You my client?" she asks.

"Oh," he says. "No."

She is startlingly pale, with purple hair.

"What are you then?"

He turns the umbrella over in his fingers. The question seems imponderable.

"I mean, what're you doing here?" She seems in a rush, poised half in, half out of the doorway like some tropical bird at its nest hole.

"Well," he says.

"You see, I've got an appointment in this room."

"Okay," he says. "That's okay. I'm just leaving."

She pats him on the shoulder on his way out the door, although it could also be interpreted as a small shove.

Halfway down the long descent of the stairwell he begins to berate himself for not asking the woman what she knew of the Filipina. He turns around, leaning over sharply at the waist.

"Excuse me," he says, breathing hard. The door is still open.

"Hey, Pops," she says.

She's smoking a cigarette, flicking the ash onto the floor.

"I was just curious. Did you know her?"

"Flora? Sure, I knew her." She grinds the butt out in the already overflowing ashtray.

Suddenly he wonders.

"Did she smoke?"

"Nope. No smokes."

"I see," he says.

"What were you?" she says as he turns to leave. "Her client?"

"No, no," he replies, turning back, steadying himself in the door frame, feeling woozy. "I wasn't anything to her. I saw her jump."

"Oh shit," she says. "What a fucked-up thing."

· · ·

At the cemetery it starts to rain. He unfurls the green umbrella from the car door. Good lord, it's gaudy, painted to look like a canopy of banana leaves. Still, it's functional.

He shuffles down the paved pathway toward the old part of the graveyard. His wife spent many happy hours here, adopting forgotten burial sites, digging out headstones from decades' worth of soil, setting them upright again. She resurrected and repainted many of the white picket fences surrounding the graves and sanded the rust off the Victorian iron railings. When he asked her what drew her here (she had no relatives buried west of the Mississippi), she said she loved the peacefulness, the way the ancient oaks and flowering shrubs marked the changing of the seasons and daffodils spread secretly underground each summer, heralding the passage of the years with an exponential population explosion each spring.

Exponential. She loved to throw mathematics back at him like that, with a mischievous glint in her eye. She had studied literature all those years ago in the college where they met, before she'd become a wife and mother. He had been her teaching assistant in an algebra class, and she'd claimed through all their marriage that her understanding of mathematics had come solely through him. Still, she frequently got it wrong and he was forced to correct her. Then she would slap him on the arm and tell him to relax. But he was what he was and didn't know what she meant by "relax."

She was always trying to engage him in projects outside his work, and she tried to enlist him in the pioneer graveyard because she needed his help, she said, lifting the heavy stones, mortaring the broken pieces back together, setting them upright in the ground. He came with her once and thought at the time that he'd tried. But now, looking back, he can see that he hadn't. He wasn't a handyman. Couldn't see how to fix things. The whole process bored him. The graveyard did not offer him peace at all, but disquiet. He dug out a few stones and lifted a few others. Yet he realizes now that he was silent and unenthusiastic and that by being so he was trying to train his wife never to ask him to come here again.

And so she didn't.

The old oaks in the cemetery are leafless now. But the winter rains have swelled the trees' shaggy coats of lichens and their patches of furlike moss, so that even without leaves they appear green and alive. Rain drips from their canopies onto the green umbrella. It's a pleasing sound. Musical, almost. Flocks of chickadees add to the cadence, *tssk*ing through the tangle of branches overhead, peeling the hulls from the buds, dropping them down like papery rain. He studies their remains on the wet toes of his old oxfords.

Ten months earlier, before the funeral, his daughter drove him to the plot for the first time, here on the far eastern edge of the grounds yet still within the stone walls of the old pioneer graveyard.

At first he thought his wife had chosen this place out of spite. She was not a spiteful woman, but maybe the illness had made her so?

"No. I don't think so," said his daughter. "I don't think that's what she had in mind at all."

Earlier that day, the day after his wife died, his daughter read the letter aloud to him as Carla held her hand in the kitchen where his wife had spent so much time. He sat on the stool with a piece of chalk in his fingers, feeling afraid. Although he wanted to write on the blackboard above the kitchen counter, he managed to refrain from actually doing so.

"It was her last plan," said his daughter, smiling weakly,

handing him the letter. "We worked on it together. She actually had a lot of fun with it."

He reread the letter silently, folded it back into thirds, and slipped it into the inner pocket of his jacket.

Apparently his wife had not trusted him to follow her wishes unsupervised?

"I don't think that was it," said his daughter. "I think she had something else in mind."

"Maybe it was just because she loved the place so much," said Carla. It seemed to him that she said it accusingly, and so he made eye contact with her for the first time that day. It always distressed him to see how pretty she was.

For the first month or so after his wife died, visiting the cemetery was like visiting a house where not long before he had grossly offended the owners. They didn't want him back. He didn't want to be there. It was unpleasant.

But that changed.

He rests now on the rock wall. He has learned to carry a plastic grocery bag to sit on, because the stones ooze dampness, even in dry weather. The green umbrella shields him from the drizzle. Alongside his wife's headstone a rangy old flowering quince is in blossom, defying the winter, its coral blossoms shuddering under the weight of raindrops falling from the trees.

How odd for him to notice such things. To notice, to remember, to visit the library later and look them up. Flowering quinces. Chickadees. The chromium carpets of wild mustard. Fermenting manzanita berries decorated with drunken flocks of cedar waxwings.

Sitting beside his wife's grave, he ponders the woman on the bridge. Again and again he comes back to the point where logic fails him. Why an umbrella? And now, why two umbrellas? Why would a woman with so few resources have two of them? He closes his eyes.

She is walking across the bridge, this prostitute. In all fairness, she has probably been forced into prostitution. A storm blows in from the Pacific and she is buffeted by the wind, yet her umbrella remains intact, perhaps because she's an expert at handling umbrellas after battling tropical monsoons. Clearly, she wants to stay dry. Cars zoom by. Water splashes up from the road. A Buick swerves toward her, possibly accelerating. She steps onto the rail. Quickly. Her umbrella snaps inside out. She pitches over and falls, swinging in graceful arcs, spiraling, she and the umbrella descending together like the paired wings of a maple seed, her eyes closed, her mouth wearing a slight smile.

However he tries to picture it, to solve it, there's always that smile of hers, which has sprouted improbably from the center of this wracked memory.

There's no formal upkeep in the old part of the graveyard. In the letter, which his daughter read aloud, his wife asked him to tend her grave. It would mean so much. He has read that part over and over again in the last months. *It would mean so much.* Not to her. She doesn't say that.

In fact, he tends her grave only intermittently. He pulls what he thinks are weeds, although if they blossom he lets them be. He allows the oak leaves to lie where they fall. Moss is growing into the engraving on her headstone, yet it seems right to him. Unlike her, he does not want to see all this restored to its Victorian primness. For the first time in his life he has come to enjoy the aura of ruin.

Still, he visits frequently. But rather than tend, he sits. It calms him. Memories come up, step across his mental screen, then exit. The going part is oddly pleasant. Sometimes equations scroll across his mind, tranquil in their mystery.

It rains and rains this winter. He carries the green umbrella everywhere. When he doesn't use it in the rain, he uses it to lean on, like a cane, or on rare days of sunshine as a parasol. Additionally, it can be used defensively to jab with (or so he imagines). Conversely, it can be turned around and used like a crook, to pull things closer.

It's a marvelous tool.

A woman from campus administration stops him and asks him where he got it, then chats for a while. His photo appears on the cover of the college newspaper, an old man bent under banana leaves. As a result he seems to develop into something of an eccentric mascot, becoming, after generations of obscurity in the Mathematics Department, almost popular. Young male students pass him in the pounding rain, their jackets pulled over their heads, shouting jovially, "Hey, Umbrella Man."

He checks on it, and because no one ever claims Flora's remains, he finally does, which means he is charged for the urn, cheap and plastic, something like a thermos. He has no idea what he's going to do with it. For several days it rolls around on the back seat of the Buick. Then he moves it inside the house, onto the laundry room shelf above the washer and dryer. But that seems wrong. He debates walking across the bridge and tossing it back into the sea.

When his daughter discovers it, he has placed it on top of the refrigerator.

"Is this a crematory urn?" she asks, incredulous.

He is startled. "Yes."

She stares at him, words forming slowly.

"Is this . . . Mom?"

"God, no." He sets his piece of chalk back into the cradle at the base of the blackboard. "Of course not."

"Oh," she says. "Someone I know?"

He lifts the urn from the refrigerator and sets it on the kitchen table. "It's Flora. The woman who jumped off the bridge."

"Flora," says Carla softly, trying out the sound of the word. Their eyes meet.

Carla nods. "No one else wanted her?" she asks.

"No," he says. "No one did."

It's still raining a month after his daughter and Carla have left for Singapore. The flowering plums have come and gone, the daffodils and crocuses are long past. He watches the maple in the cemetery heave slender arms, its tiny new leaves sailing hard at anchor. Spring has added bluster to the storms, and birds whip across the sky as if flung from slingshots.

The new season has given him a sense of levity he's never felt before. Sitting with his wife, he can feel the wind probing his jacket and under the rim of his hat. His thoughts have become lighter too, whisking across his mind. He no longer follows where they go.

With the aid of the umbrella, he pushes himself off the stone wall and leans back, staring up. The old oak's buds are beginning to unfurl.

He is strolling back to his car, pondering an elliptic equation, when a gust of wind sweeps through, so strong that it carries twigs and litter with it. When he raises his arms to shield his face, his hat flips away, and he spins and tries to grab it. Too late. The long legs buckle. His balance is gone, and dust fills his eyes. He is going over. But just as he falls, he feels himself float. He would swear to it. Eyes closed, he finds himself smiling.

Darwin in Heaven

C HARLES DARWIN STUMBLED upon evidence of God's
happiness soon after his arrival in heaven, while still in a tour-
ist-abroad state of mind: overexcited, underrested, struggling
with a new diet and foreign languages. Despite these dif-
ficulties, he took copious notes, albeit not on paper. He discovered that he had only to talk, or even to think, and these
thoughts sounded themselves out in a range of musical voices
as if a choir were singing his ideas. At first this alarmed him:
the idea that angels were heralding his *scribbles.* He felt the
need to wait and further organize his thoughts, at least into a
rough draft. But when he listened closely, he could hear that
heaven was awaft with these sighing, humming offertories. Everyone had them. He could even tune in to them if he wanted,
and sometimes he did. To Socrates, whose thinking on the natural world had taken startling turns in the last 2,300 years. To
Lao-Tzu, whose voice, unbidden, came to Darwin like a calm-
ing sip of tea.

In a misty, windswept realm of heaven, Darwin first experienced God's joy. The place wore the dampness of the inside of clouds. He recognized the guayavita bushes with berries and the long pale-green filamentous lichens hanging in tresses from the boughs of the trees. All just as he remembered from the Galápagos Islands. Suddenly he understood. This was Tortoise Heaven, complete with deliciously muddy wallowing pools, succulent cactuses, high-altitude springs, and a network of trails worn into the ghost volcanoes by an infinitude of slow-motion travelers, the upward-bound tortoises with their necks outstretched, anticipating water, the downward-bound with their necks outstretched, imagining cactus. Arriving here, Darwin felt a heavy joy settle into his chest and jotted a preliminary observation into his mental notebook: mercy × eternity = happiness.

Since then, Darwin's self-appointed task has been to understand the origin of God's happiness. Is His felicity the spark of life or simply the smoke from its already burning fires? The former would imply that God's master plan was a jubilee from the start. The latter, that God had only stumbled upon joy in the course of creation. The subject interests Darwin because, aside from his time aboard the *Beagle*, wandering and exploring, happiness was a feeling that eluded him during much of his life on earth, and even in heaven it comes to him only intermittently. He wonders if he must likewise stumble upon it or if its seed is already within him.

This search is the monumental task Darwin has been working on for his 122 years here. Not that years matter in heaven. Still, Darwin is a scientist. He keeps track of these things. In the beginning, dumbstruck by the existence of heaven and by his own presence here, Darwin did little actual work. Those were exceedingly pleasant times, visiting all of heaven's realms, making notes and drawings, letting perfect ideas slip through the fingers of his mind. He felt he was making progress in those days, and even began to toy with a theory. But he remains a painstakingly methodical man, just as he was on earth, never giving shape to nebulous thoughts until forced to.

Or until the competition heats up. Which could have happened in 1955, when Albert Einstein arrived. But even then Darwin refrained from feeling pressured. From his point of view, if Einstein's answer to the origin of God's happiness was anything like $E = mc^2$, then he didn't care. He never could understand mathematics, on earth or in heaven. The problem — the ticking clock, so to speak — began in 1988, with the appearance of Richard P. Feynman. This man worries Darwin, with his Nobel Prize in physics and his ferociously roving mind that straddles subjects and scientific fields like a giant. Yet Feynman is a man who will also lie down on the ground to observe ants. He questions everything, takes no answer as gospel, and broadcasts his own results with evangelical charm and charisma. His book, *Surely You're Joking, Mr. Feynman,* was a masterpiece of entertainment and explanation on earth, spending countless weeks on the *New York Times* bestseller list. Whereas Darwin's writing, by his own admission, leads him to fog the clarity of the English language at every clause.

And now, even in heaven, even in the absence of bestseller lists, Feynman's ideas resound rampantly through the ether, driving Darwin to distraction. But what really unnerves him is Feynman's deep taproot of humor, a quality noticeably absent from Darwin's own character. Feynman's laughter, his omnipresent chuckle from within, is, Darwin suspects, something closely akin to God's happiness. Fearful that he has squandered his 106-year head start, Darwin is forced into feverish action, composing his ideas into small operettas, which he arranges and rearranges in the air around him with obsessive unease: *The Origin of God, or the Race for the Preservation of the Favored Scientist in the Struggle for the Afterlife.*

It's at best, he knows, a working title.

As he did when voyaging aboard the *Beagle,* Darwin spends much of his time with the giant tortoises. But as it turns out, so do many others. Even here the Galápagos tortoises are beloved, and many people who couldn't make the pilgrimage on earth do so in heaven, forcing Darwin (reluctantly) into the position of a tour guide. Perched on a lava boulder near a freshwater spring where the tortoises come to drink, he finds himself repeatedly answering the same simplistic questions.

"See how they sink their heads above their eyes in the water," he explains to the eager crowds. "If you measure their rate, you'll see that it's ten gulps a minute."

When (invariably) a ghost asks, "Did you discover that here or on earth?" Darwin snaps back, "Don't you read? Didn't they teach you anything in school?" He can't help it. Toward the end of his life, utterly reviled for his theory of evolution, he took comfort from the company of orchids and earthworms. He still has difficulty trusting people.

At times he gets the tortoises to himself. Late in the heavenly night, for instance, when most other ghosts visit earth (Darwin does not). These are his best times, as the tortoises are invariably affectionate, stretching out their necks for a rub, hissing softly. Trudging slowly through their corner of heaven, they tenderly step aside for small things in their way while letting large forces, such as floods, flow over them. They talk to each other in the universal language whispering through the air, and Darwin loves their thoughts: serene reflections devoid of hurry or worry, utterly lacking in conflict. He notices that they neither interpret nor judge, simply mirror their world in such a way that a tortoise informing another that a fire ant is crawling across its head and is perhaps about to inflict a painful bite will simply say, *Fire ant dwells too, on tortoise.* They remind Darwin of Lao-Tzu, who, tortoiselike, spent much of his life alone in a cave:

> Manifest plainness,
> Embrace simplicity,
> Reduce selfishness,
> Have few desires.

Late one night a Harley-Davidson comes roaring up the wide tortoise trails. The tortoises hear it before Darwin does and yank their heads from the springs, water dripping down the folds of their necks. Darwin sighs and settles himself into a sagelike position on a lava boulder, preparing himself for the usual queries. As the ghost parks his bike, Darwin notices the bumper sticker. It's the Darwin fish, with legs upside down. On earth, Darwin knows, there's a fish war under way, and this particular design, belonging to the Christians, would say, *Darwin Is Dead.* But this upside-down fish sports a halo and the words *Darwin's in Heaven.*

"You gotta love it," says the ghost, dismounting from the bike, his huge frontal lobe wrinkling in delight as he rubs the sticker clean. "One hundred and thirty-one years later and they're still debating it."

With a sinking feeling, Darwin realizes who this is. "Evolution?" he asks faintly.

"Yeah," says Richard P. Feynman. "You're like Christ. Or

the Buddha. You'll live forever through sheer controversy."

"Well," says Darwin, "we're all living forever anyway. Aren't we?"

Feynman laughs. It's a snort followed by a guffaw, tapering off into a giggle. Definitely a nerd laugh. But not one of derision, one of joyful inquiry. "Are we?" he asks, hands waving through the air. "What makes you think so?"

Oh. The endless questions, the questioning of all authority. Darwin feels it ignite his heartburn.

"I knew I'd find you here," says Feynman.

"You did?"

"Sure. And you knew I'd come, didn't you?"

Darwin laughs nervously. "Of course," he says, lying.

Feynman reaches out to pat a tortoise, which, Darwin jealously notes, hisses pleasantly.

"Any new thinking on them?" says Feynman. "Now that you've been here awhile?"

The question alarms Darwin. It's like asking him to sing and dance when he can't do either, and certainly not unrehearsed. Feynman apparently reads his mind, for out of thin air materializes a set of bongo drums, which he attacks like a gorilla. Darwin has read about this in Feynman's book, his bongo *talents*. It's another aspect of the man that worries Darwin, who doesn't have a musical bone in his body but suspects that God is melody and harmony all at once.

"Hey," shouts Feynman above the din. "I think the tortoises like it."

The tortoises are listening with their eyes closed.

"Actually," shouts Darwin, "they do that when they're annoyed."

Feynman stops drumming. "How do you know?"

"They're retreating. In the tortoise way. Inside themselves."

"Why don't they just leave?" says Feynman, sweat dripping down his oversized forehead.

"Because they're more patient than you. They know you'll leave first."

"Are you sure?"

"Am I sure you'll leave first? Or that they're annoyed?"

"Touché," says Feynman, who then turns to the tortoises. "Did you like it?"

Long moments of silence pass. Feynman taps the drum. "Did — you — enjoy — it?" he repeats, sounding each word loudly.

Darwin finds that *he's* enjoying it. Tortoises, he knows, are polite beyond human imagination.

"Hey!" shouts Feynman. *"Did you dig it?"*

One tortoise turns slowly toward him and opens her eyes, her expression pure benevolence.

"Ah-hah," says Feynman. "Ah-hah."

"Ah-hah what?"

"Just what I thought," says Feynman. "They loved it."

After this, Darwin realizes that Feynman too is prey to human weaknesses and the race may not be as uneven as he first thought. Even so, he has to stop himself from constantly monitoring Feynman, to see where in heaven the man's got to (everywhere, it seems) and what he's questioning now (the sunlight, is it real? the ghosts, are they really dead?). For a while, unfortunately, Darwin does just this, becomes the cosmic equivalent of a couch potato tuned in to the Feynman channel. But after continual prodding from his ghostly conscience, he remembers that he must live his own afterlife, not Richard P. Feynman's.

He decides to focus on an area where he has already made

some progress, where he's got that all-important jump start, and returns to Bat Heaven, a dark and damp corner of the realm where light never enters, has *never* entered, yet where happiness lies as thick as an eternity's worth of guano as bat laughter pings off the cave walls. Why are bats happy? Surely he never suspected this on earth. In fact he never took much account of bats, other than a passing interest in the vampire bats of Brazil. But here, sitting in the darkness, he can feel their happiness like an ether, a combustible gas ripe to explode.

"What?" asks Darwin over and over again. "What's so funny?"

"Listen," say the bats.

He listens. Their laughter, which earth scientists thought was echolocational and therefore for navigation only, is as weightless and fractional as light. It *is* light, Darwin realizes, in an auditory kind of way, as if a billion tiny Tinkerbells were afloat in the cave.

He closes his eyes. It's no darker than before, but somehow this enables him to let the laughter into his ears. It tickles. He never realized that before. Ha. Ultrasound like microfingers on his eardrums. Ha. What a *peculiar* sensation. Ha-ha-ha. Now he hears something else. A strange sound, deep and choking, coming from his own insides. It's Darwin laughter, something he hasn't heard in longer than he can remember. How strange. It grabs at his guts and blasts outward like a cough.

He is, he realizes, out of practice. This fact seems deliriously funny. He stumbles for the cave exit.

"There's more," say the bats.

"I can't take any more," says Darwin, shaking, doubled over with laughter.

"The problem is, you're oriented the wrong way," say the bats.

Whatever it means, it's absurdly, grotesquely funny. Darwin falls to the floor and rolls. He snorts with laughter.

"You must get upside down," say the bats.

He can't breathe, not even ghost breath. Laughter heehaws in and out of his chest. The pain is unbearable. He can hardly speak. "How," he splutters, "do I do that?"

Whump.

Miracle. That's how it goes in heaven.

Just like that, a set of monkey bars is in the cave and Darwin is hanging upside down from the knees. His arms bobble loosely from the shoulders, rubbing against his ears. His lips fall open and his hair releases from the roots to stand up, or rather down. He looks, he realizes, like a fool. The mental image of himself is overwhelming, and he prepares himself for the next onslaught of laughter. But even as it comes, one small corner of Darwin's scientist's brain continues to work.

Amazing. Upside down, with gravity reversed, laughter becomes the force of something running downhill, like a river. Liberated, it causes no pain.

He laughs and laughs. It even sounds different, higher and lighter, pinging around the cave and bouncing off the walls, mirth without cause or effect. To top it off, swaying as he is upside down, he feels the relief of his spine adjusting itself, one vertebra after another. Pop, pop, pop, pop.

Now he's in a quandary. There's no doubt about it. He's made one of those foundational discoveries, something upon which a great pyramid of thought could be built. *Happiness is effortless.* But the problem is, he can't afford to think about it. If he does, those (damned) angels will trumpet forth his thoughts for all to hear, including of course Richard P. Feynman.

Still, he can't control himself. So he tries to mask the inevitable musings, to encode them if possible. *God* — (I'm not thinking about anything) *must* — (is that a hair in my soup?) *live* — (where is the left sock?) *upside* — (my mind is a total blank) *down.*

It's a terrible way to work and not one that comes naturally to Darwin. But he must adapt. Darwin knows this: adapt or perish.

He finds, however, that he can't hide his revelation from the tortoises, whose carapaces, like huge conch shells or giant ears, are attuned to even the slightest vibrations of the cosmos.

"You're aquiver, Charles," says one to him when they're alone one night.

"Mmm?" says Darwin.

"Yes. You're oscillating," says another.

"Oh," says Darwin. "Something I ate?"

All the tortoises turn toward him and close their eyes. They hear everything, even the slight sibilance of condensation as the mist settles into dew on the hanging lichen fronds.

"I believe you're excited," says a tortoise after a lengthy silence.

"Really?" says Darwin, trying to remain nonchalant. The tortoises open their eyes to study him, and Darwin finds himself squirming under their placid gazes. "Well," he says, "it might be that. I mean, it could be. It's possible. Ha. Ha-ha." But he can't really laugh, because his stomach muscles are still sore from what transpired in the bat cave.

Suddenly the voice of Lao-Tzu comes to him, as it always does, like a breeze, mysterious and unbidden.

The Way of Heaven has no favorites.

"Did you hear that?" says Darwin.

He finds it to be a pleasant thought. But is it true? (It certainly disrupts the working title of his thesis.) And if it isn't true? If there *are* favorites and Darwin abandons the race, then he will be — what? — left behind in the struggle for God's favor. Trampled over. Intellectually extinct. As if to punctuate this thought, the din of Feynman's bongos suddenly punches through his musings, each percussive beat assailing him like a body blow until he is actually reeling: to the left, doubled over, backward.

"Charles," says a tortoise, "other answers lie in the sea."

Darwin puts down his fists, comes to a stop, panting.

"Ctenophores," says another.

The very idea worries him.

Water is another one of Darwin's weak suits. Although he was perfectly happy aboard the *Beagle* watching frothy swells smack against the bow, then roll down the length of the hull, the thought of getting into this watery realm is a decidedly unpleasant one. Still, he trusts the tortoises. But what does one do with one's arms and legs? How does one breathe? In heaven, of course, these questions are moot, yet even so he enters the ocean one toe at a time, goosebumpy and self-conscious in his nineteenth-century bathing costume. Once he is submerged, it's not that bad. He doesn't have to swim or breathe and can simply will himself ahead with his mind's propellers.

Onward he goes, into the bottomless blue of the pelagic zone, where shafts of sunlight pierce the crystalline water and converge into a liquid vanishing point hundreds of feet beneath him. Here he stops, faces the light, instinctively dog-paddling. He lets the current wash over him, refixes the focus of his eyes in order to see a few inches in front of his nose.

There they are. Tiny, transparent spheres the size of grapes,

ribbed with fused cilia: their combs, which beat and beat —
pulse, really — carrying them millimeter by millimeter across
the infinity of heaven's ocean. The ctenophores, or comb jellies.

Darwin is hypnotized. He observes as the ribs of their
combs gather and refract the light, casting tiny rainbows as
ethereal as stardust. They trail long, adhesive tentacles like
fishing lures, which they are. He can see inside them to where
some are carrying their latest meals, the red pearls of colonial
salps or a larval fish. If he holds up his hand as a backdrop, he
can just make out the greenish streaks of the ctenophores' in-
terior glandular structures, streaks that turn bioluminescent at
night.

He finds himself at a loss as to how to speak to an inverte-
brate plankton. It is, after all, little more than organized, ani-
mate seawater.

"That's exactly the point," he hears.

Who said that? He spins in the water, ctenophores brushing
by him.

"What point?" says Darwin.

"The seawater point." The voice comes from everywhere, yet
nowhere.

"You mean that you're just living seawater?" says Darwin,
looking up, then down, unsure of where to direct his gaze as he
tries to make eye contact with an eyeless ctenophore.

"What are you?" says the voice.

"Human, of course."

"Mostly water?"

"Yes. You could say that."

"Saltwater?"

He gets the point.

"No," say the ctenophores. "You think you understand, but you don't."

Darwin rolls his eyes, then sighs. "All right. What point?"

A small parade of them bobs past his nose, but none answers.

Darwin finds himself suddenly swatting at the water, as if the ctenophores were flies. Such annoying little creatures. But they only somersault away in the wash from his hands.

"What point?" says Darwin, loudly.

They're so soft and yielding, swaying like fluid within fluid. The beating cilia of their combs don't actually propel them, only maintain their orientation in the water as they travel, mouths forward. Rainbows of light pulse up and down their sides. He must admit, they're as lovely as fairies.

Within an instant of this thought, the sea turns black and the sky is dark and filled with stars. Darwin gasps, terrified to be alone in the nighttime sea. His pique and bravado have left him, and he freezes, motionless, wishing he were anywhere but in the temperamental realm of Jellyfish Heaven.

"Scientist," say the ctenophores, "swat away."

"Swat?" he whispers.

"As you were before."

Darwin pretends to wave a hand through the water but really just wiggles his fingers.

"Your hands," say the jellies.

Tentatively he pushes one fist away from the shelter of his body, then brings it quickly back again.

"Harder," they say.

Lord, what obnoxious life forms. Darwin goes after them with vigor, swatting and swiping, grabbing with his hands, hoping to flatten a few. But as if by magic his hands are glowing, ablaze with the explosive sparkle of fireworks. Long trails of iridescent blue-green mark the path of his arms through the water. He kicks his legs and the sea catches fire, as bright as neon, highlighting every eddy, every plume of motion. It's simply incredible. He swims, turning his head to watch the streams of light and motion blossom like a cosmic peacock tail in the water behind him.

"It's your bioluminescence?" he says.

"Not all ours," say the jellies. "The dinoflagellates are here too."

Darwin has never felt anything like it before. In the presence of this light — no, not just the presence, in the course of *activating* this wondrous light, he is enveloped in something that feels like pure joy.

"Wrong again, human," say the jellies. "It's not the activating, it's the *being activated* that's joyful."

He doesn't care. Their magic is so delightful that they can no longer irritate him and can taunt him all they want, these brainless, eyeless pixies. He'll think about what they mean later. For now, he'll do nothing more than cavort in their intoxicating sea of bliss.

After this Darwin begins to get careless. He can't help it. There's so much data to process, so much exciting fodder, and he can't always remember to mask it with banalities so that Richard P. Feynman won't listen in. Darwin tries to do his deepest thinking at night, when most ghosts are occupied.

With the tortoises sitting quietly beside him, he lets his eyes rest on the earth below, half light, half dark. *So God too must glow in the dark.*

Suddenly there's an explosion in front of him, a candle

bomb of spitting yellow-orange light. From behind it emerges a figure in a black cape with a black mask over its eyes.

"I always wanted to be a magician," says Richard P. Feynman.

Coughing, waving the smoke from his face, Darwin finds himself wondering if the devil exists after all.

"You gotta admit, heaven's a gas," says Feynman.

"You're happy, aren't you?" says Darwin, methodically flicking burning embers off his tweed jacket.

"Sure. I'm delirious. You're not?"

Darwin shrugs.

"Porque, hombre?" says Feynman. "All the answers are here. Everything we always wondered about on earth. And by the sound of it, you're getting to the bottom of a few. The upside-down thing, the bioluminescent thing."

Darwin flinches.

"It's good solid work, Charles. What are you ashamed of?"

"Ashamed? I'm not ashamed." But his face is flushed, and he feels his scalp prickling. Why is this ghost haunting him?

"What are *you* working on?" Darwin asks, expecting Feynman to dissemble, or to disappear.

"Like you," says Feynman, rubbing his hands. "The big stuff. God."

Darwin blinks. "What about God?"

"Is there a God?"

Darwin is shocked. *Is there a God?* How can one be in heaven and question such a thing? The man's a heretic.

"Hey, it's not such a weird question. I mean, have you seen God?" Feynman raises his caped arm across his face, affects a Bela Lugosi accent. "Where the hell is He? Or She. Why is It hiding?"

Flash.

Just like that, Richard P. Feynman is gone without a trace. Darwin wonders whether this is just another part of the man's theatrics or evidence of divine wrath.

But the question has inserted itself like a tick in Darwin's skin, bloating with each passing day. Rather than energizing him, it saps his afterlife-blood. Why think, if there's no God? Why work? It's all so insoluble. Increasingly, Darwin does nothing but loll in puddles of sunshine up in Tortoise Heaven, hiding from and ignoring the visiting ghosts, imagining that he himself has grown a tortoise carapace into which he will retreat. Forever.

For ages and ages Charles Darwin lives as a tortoise, happily surrounded by tortoises, content within their silence, sharing their simple contemplations as they methodically chew heaven's infinite supply of sweet and succulent plants. Into this seclusion one day comes another message from Lao-Tzu.

> One may know the world without going out of doors.
> One may see the Way of Heaven without looking
> through the windows.

Good. This suits Darwin fine. He uses the dictum to pat himself on the back, to congratulate himself for doing nothing. But as so often happens with Lao-Tzu's messages, the statement arouses its opposite, and as the days go by the message begins to ripple, to tip all the latent questions Darwin has been holding in stasis until they cascade like dominoes, forcing him to move, one foot after the other, out the door of Tortoise Heaven.

Darwin finds Lao-Tzu in a cave high on a mountain, where he can tell the man comes and goes by the half-melted trails in the snow. But when Darwin arrives, Lao-Tzu will not come out, will not let Darwin in, will speak with him only from the shadows.

"Why are you sending me messages?" says Darwin.

"Am I?" says the voice from the darkness.

A long silence ensues.

Darwin sits in the snow, shielding his eyes with a hand. The glare up here is painful. He tries to peer into the cave, but the contrast between light and dark is too great.

"Have *you* seen God?" asks Darwin.

More silence.

"Don't you read?" says the voice within the cave.

This is Darwin's line to the tourists in Tortoise Heaven. Only Lao-Tzu says it without accusation.

"What should I reread?" says Darwin, as gently as he can manage.

"The Four Eternal Models," says Lao-Tzu. After that, he will say nothing more. So Darwin slowly retraces his steps down the snowy mountainside, trying to remember how the Four Eternal Models begins. *Before the Heaven and Earth existed . . .*

Just as he reaches the treeline he spins quickly and looks back. Outside the cave is a tiny figure silhouetted against the snow. It flinches a little, recognizing that it has been seen, and Darwin finds himself momentarily ashamed for having exposed the sage. But then Lao-Tzu begins to wave a tiny arm high in the air, vigorous and enthusiastic, delighted to be saying goodbye.

As if some other hand is directing him, Darwin journeys toward a corner of the realm he has never visited before, one so ancient and empty that until now it seemed superfluous to his studies.

> Before the Heaven and Earth existed
> There was something nebulous.

It's a low-contour world, just a flat shoreline and the horizontal sweep of the ocean's horizon. Black pillows of stony material rise a few feet above the shallow water near shore. Farther out, they form pillars. Darwin recognizes them. Stromatolites. The limestone secretions of the earth's first photosynthesizing organisms: the blue-green algae, or cyanophytes. Two billion years ago blue-greens evolved on earth and changed life forever. By separating the hydrogen from the oxygen in water, by using the hydrogen as their food and then releasing the oxygen into the air, the blue-greens inadvertently (or not?) created the atmosphere for all the life that would follow.

It's a peaceful place, Blue-Green Heaven. The sunshine is warm, massaging the ripples on the surface of the water as Darwin wades through the shallows. This is the simplest world imaginable. Nothing else is yet alive here — no crabs, no stingrays, no schools of sergeant-majors, not even limpets or sea urchins. Yet Darwin can feel the potential, the promise of a virile future.

> I do not know its name
> And address it as Tao.
> If forced to give it a name, I shall call it "Great."

It all makes sense. He can feel the pieces of ideas falling into order, into that preordained, elegant shape that truth invariably takes. He sits in the water, bent over, head submerged, feeling a kind of humming: the sound of production, of transformation, of sunlight turning into life. It's a sound so under-stated, so low-key, that he realizes if he had only listened, he would have heard it pulsing throughout both heaven and earth from the beginning.

> Being great implies reaching out in space,
> Reaching out in space implies far-reaching,
> Far-reaching implies reversion to the original point.

He feels a splash beside him but is reluctant to remove his head from the source of this sound. When he turns to look, he sees Richard P. Feynman beside him under water, grinning wildly.

"You realize what you've got?" says Feynman, bubbles rising from his mouth.

Darwin nods.

"It's the Source," says Feynman.

Darwin smiles.

Feynman claps Darwin on the shoulder. "It all comes from here. Or something like here."

"Or else, being circular, it comes from anywhere along the curve."

"Or everywhere, all at once," says Feynman. "Like the curvature of space."

"Better yet," says Darwin.

They absorb the humming.

"So. You think God's a blue-green?" says Feynman.

"Among other things," says Darwin.

In its utter simplicity, Blue-Green Heaven is rich beyond measure. Feynman and Darwin wade through the tidepools, float on their backs in the salty water, and let the sunlight tattoo their skin. Buoyant and warm, the place is deeply conducive to accessing the preconscious parts of the brain, and here, Darwin finds his mind surrendering the questions.

Time passes, but only on earth.

"Gotta go," says Feynman after an eon or two.

They've barely spoken until now.

"So soon?" says Darwin.

"I'm going back to earth. This is only a start."

Darwin, floating on his back, notices the small clouds collecting in the direction of the sunset, as they always seem to do. He could ask why, but for the moment, at least, doesn't.

"Ah," he says. "What will you be?"

"A phycologist."

"Of course," says Darwin. "Algae or seaweeds?"

"Algae," says Feynman. "I think I'll be an astrophycologist. Visit other worlds."

"Are they doing that now?" says Darwin, swishing his hands lazily through the water.

"Yup."

"Good for them."

"Of course, you can't guarantee that what you want *here* will happen *there*," says Feynman.

"Course not," says Darwin.

"I mean, I could end up a plumber."

"There are algae everywhere," says Darwin.

Feynman laughs. "Good one, Charles."

Darwin stays on after Feynman leaves, enjoying the pleasures of an empty mind. When he does think, his thoughts spiral outward to return gentled by their spacious journey. Over time, his untroubled musings crack open the seed of an idea. Perhaps the human intellect is not a gift so much as a challenge to overcome, and if not for its questing, earth and heaven would merge.

Eventually, Charles Darwin returns to Tortoise Heaven, and to his delight, the humming of the blue-green algae comes with him. He hears it in the breath of the giant tortoises, in the whispers of fog, and in the thud of hiking boots on tortoise trails as the tourists trek up to visit.

"Did you discover that here or in the Galápagos?" they ask about this or that.

"It all comes from here," he says mildly. "Even if you found it there."

Meanwhile he works on his thesis, slowly and without pressure, making notes, drawing drawings, letting perfect ideas slip easily through his mind. *God's Happiness as Manifest in All Things, Dead, Alive, and Extinct! And How to Find It for Yourself.* He has toyed with a simpler title: *Bliss.* But he finds himself enjoying his newest realization, that heaven embraces the unwieldy and the imperfect too.

Occasionally he checks in on Richard P. Feynman, now going by the name of Iris Singh, who at age six is already showing a remarkable predilection for drumming and drives her parents into alternating fits of pride and horror at her pursuit of noise. Darwin could console them with the knowledge that any day now little Iris will discover the pond on Agricultural Deck 7B of their ship, where the spirulina is grown. But he decides to let them spin through space toward their own startling destinies.

Stealing from the Dead

AUGUSTA HALE DECIDED to hear Bedford de Banville-Hughes speak because she was in Venice and Lord Byron seemed to be someone she should learn more about. Not that she knew of Mr. de Banville-Hughes or his book, *The Aphrodisia of a Romantic Poet: Lord Byron and the Impossible Passions of the Nineteenth Century.* But she was hungry to hear her own language. THE HIGH-WATER MARK OF A ROMANTIC POET, the poster advertised in cheap inks that were beginning to bleed in the rain. Augusta was sure it hadn't been there the night before when she'd leaned against this same wall trying to escape the drizzle. Now she had an umbrella with her, a bony black model with broken tines that she used to joust at the weather, which seemed to seep from below as well as pour from above in Venice.

She arrived twenty minutes late for the lecture, having impulsively skipped her evening fresco restoration class at the Università Internazionale dell'Arte. Bedford de Banville-Hughes was also late. Augusta noticed that he took the podium at exactly the moment she dropped her painting box on the floor and took her seat. The synchronicity aroused her interest, and she studied him in the moment before he spoke as he adjusted the microphone and sipped from a glass of water. His eyes seemed femininely beautiful, and his body a little too long but graceful.

"I give you Byron's salute to Italy," he said.

> *I love the language, that soft bastard Latin,*
> *Which melts like kisses from a female mouth.*

Pausing to look up from his papers, de Banville-Hughes caught Augusta's eye and smiled. She smiled back, that all-important first smile. Of late she'd been trying out a version of Leonardo's *Cecilia Gallarani,* the half-smile, the head turned away.

De Banville-Hughes whipped a page off his lectern and tossed it to the stage behind him. "A dramatic opening," he said, "for a man who caressed drama from the mundane in life."

For the rest of the evening Augusta caught only snatches of his words, particularly the ones that were sent her way with a glance: *A little she strove, and much repented, / And whispering 'I will ne'er consent' — consented.* Excitement flashed from under heavy lids as he looked out at the audience. *Pleasure's a sin,* he quoted, *and sometimes sin's a pleasure.* A thought rose in Augusta's mind: *I could love him.*

De Banville-Hughes leaned down to rest his chin on his hand, his gaze sweeping across the audience of wet *studenti* in their folding chairs with puddles of rainwater under them. Augusta felt his eyes linger on her.

"Byron was aggressive in romance. To him, it was not something to be saved and hoarded. He insisted on spending it every day. There was no bank account of moderation for Lord Byron. No pension for future days of rationality."

> *Let joy be unconfined;*
> *No sleep till morn, when Youth and Pleasure meet*
> *To chase the glowing Hours with flying fleet.*

Augusta led the standing ovation at the conclusion of his lecture. Afterward she waited in the line of admirers to buy his book. Fluffing her curls with her fingers, she was pleased to notice the Italian men in line admiring her and believed it to be incredibly fortuitous that her hair should be so auburn here in the city of Titian.

"The name, signorina?" de Banville-Hughes asked with a British clip when Augusta reached the front of the line. His fingers were delicate and white, befitting a writer, his pen poised over the title page of her copy of his book.

"Augusta Hale," she said.

"American?" he said, looking up.

She nodded.

"Any relation to Nathan?"

She began her customary assent (even though there was actually no proof of any family connection to Nathan Hale), then remembered that the British regarded him not as a patriot but as a spy. "No," she said. "Not at all."

"Too bad," said de Banville-Hughes with a regretful smile. "It would spice up the family tree, wouldn't it?"

Augusta mentally kicked herself.

"Byron, as I'm sure you know," said de Banville-Hughes, "greatly admired the fathers of the American Revolution." Augusta nodded as if she knew this, though her attention was on an invasive thought: if she waited outside and grabbed him by his wayward blond hair and kissed him passionately, he would be subsumed by her romantic fervor and compelled to make love to her behind the curtains of a gondola as the gondolier thrust them forward with an oar and an aria. *And up and down the long canals they go,* de Banville-Hughes had read, *And under the Rialto shoot along.* She'd had precious little romance in this city of love since she had arrived, half a year ago.

He scribbled something on the page. "Molto grazie, Signorina Hale," he said, and handed her back the book. "Next?"

She flew to the privacy of a bathroom stall to read what he'd written:

> To Augusta Hale —
> Who like Byron's Italia "hast the fatal gift of beauty."
> Venice is brightened by your charms.
>> B de Banville-Hughes
>> Hotel Accademia–Villa Maravegie

Augusta snapped the book closed. Did he want her to come by his room? Of course he did. Why else would he have written his hotel there? But what if he didn't and she showed up? He was probably twice her age. And married. Or gay. But did he want her, and when? Tonight? It was still only dinnertime. Should she be waiting in his room when he returned from his doubtlessly jovial, intellectually stimulating, victorious meal? Oysters from Chioggia? Spaghetti alle vongole? A bowl of Venetian brodetto? Would he bring her back a tiramisù and a glass of pinot bianco? Should she be waiting naked, like the famous Venetian courtesans of old? Or artistically nude, like the Venus of Urbino? No. Absurd. What *did* he want?

She decided to visit him but not that night. Instead she returned to her tiny bed-sit on the Calle di Gesu e Maria, a cramped, mildewy room that smelled of must and mothballs and was relieved only by the two massive floor-to-ceiling windows that flooded the space with light and provided a tiny fragment of a view of the Grand Canal. Augusta lit a stick of incense and sat on the horsehair mattress of her small iron bed with de Banville-Hughes's book propped on her knees, searching his chapter on *Don Juan* for clues:

> *Juan seem'd*
> *To her, as 'twere, the kind of being sent,*
> *Of whom these two years she had nightly dream'd,*
> *A something to be loved, a creature meant*
> *To be her happiness.*

The next morning she visited Titian's *Madonna di Ca' Pesaro* at the Church of the Frari. This madonna's face was based on Titian's wife's and reflected little of the ecstasy common among the mothers of Christ. To Augusta's eye, she didn't appear in the least thrilled at her placement midway between heaven and earth.

At the Ponte della Donna Onesta, Augusta paused. The heavy weather was lifting. Pearls of light spilled from fractured clouds, and the canal rocked with opaline waves. Water was the palette of Venice, the liquid mirrors reflecting pink stucco, cerulean skies, chrome-yellow domes, and the deep, pellucid shadows of mauve and umber. Augusta hesitated, shifting her painting box from one shoulder to the other, her fingers itching to make color. Instead she continued on to the Hotel Accademia–Villa Maravegie.

He was not in the breakfast room when she arrived, but then, she had planned to be there before him. She took a table by the windows overlooking the garden, where an ancient Chinese wisteria drooped languid clusters of violet flowers. The Grand Canal lay beyond the garden gate. Vaporetti chugged by and fleets of gondolas ferried parties of Japanese tourists across from the Piazza San Marco. She ordered cappuccino and a chocolate brioche, then turned her eyes to the dining room door.

He came in one hour and twenty-seven minutes later, half an hour after Augusta had begun to resent him and fifteen minutes after she had decided to leave (although she reminded herself that he could hardly know she was waiting). Still, she'd drunk three cappuccinos, which increased her anxiety, and read the *International Herald-Tribune* from front to back. Worst of all, she'd watched the limpid light go out of the morning as the clouds obscured even the pewter glint that saved most overcast Venice days. *Paintless,* she thought, *a paintless day.*

He was alone, which was a relief. But he failed to notice her and sat across the room in profile, shaking open a newspaper, lighting a cigarette, and sipping from a tiny glass of espresso. How best to make her presence known? Should she march up to him and pose seductively? Drop something? Call loudly for the waiter? Faint?

"Mr. de Banville-Hughes," she said, clutching her painting box in front of her. "Good morning. I'm so sorry to interrupt you."

He looked up with a myopic frown. Celadon, she thought. His eyes were celadon green, fringed with black lashes.

"Yes?"

She fumbled her grip on the canvas painting box.

"I remember," he said. "Miss Hale. Right?"

She nodded.

"Have a seat." He stood quickly, jerking a chair away for her.

"You can call me Augusta."

"Apparently, Augusta," he said, indicating his newspaper, "Venice is not only sinking, it's rotting."

"I'm sorry?" she said.

"Well, it says here that the canals, which used to be cleaned once a decade, have not been cleaned in more than thirty years."

"Is that a problem?" asked Augusta softly. Clearly he was nervous.

"If they don't drain the canals to clean and repair the foundations of the buildings, then they'll just fall apart. It's only a matter of time. I mean, the question really going through my mind is, would Byron swim in them if he were alive today?" He looked hard into her eyes, as if she knew the answer. "And then on top of it all, nobody actually remembers how to drain the canals."

"I see," said Augusta. She took her painting box off her lap and placed it on the floor beside her. "I think Italians are like Byron," she said, remembering his lecture. "You know, 'no pension for future days of sanity,' or however you put it."

A smile spread across his features. His skin actually changed tone. She'd pleased him, and tried to imagine which colors she would mix to reflect this new complexion, but she could only picture the golden luminescence of light in Bellini's painting *Saint Francis in Ecstasy*.

"Well, now," he said reappraisingly, "how lovely of you to remember." She smiled, the sweet, knowing smile of Botticelli's

Venus. "Are you a painter, Augusta?" he asked, tilting his head toward her box on the floor.

She flushed, shrugging her shoulders and tossing a wave of hair behind an ear. "I'm trying," she said.

"You know, Byron wrote quite wonderfully of the isolation of art: *I stood / Among them, but not of them; in a shroud / Of thoughts which were not their thoughts.*"

"Actually," said Augusta, "I'm studying art restoration."

"Oh, don't!" said de Banville-Hughes, leaning in close.

His eyes weren't pure celadon, she realized, but flecked with gold. "Don't?" she said.

"Don't restore," he said. "It's all the Italians do these days. You must create your own visions."

"Oh," said Augusta, blushing.

"Make your own paintings," he said. "Don't settle for mimicry."

A waiter came by and emptied the ashtray into his apron as de Banville-Hughes rose. "It was such a pleasure seeing you again, Augusta." She took the long white hand floating in front of her. He was leaving, already? How could he? Was she too young, too cloying? His handshake was wispy, which made her want to squeeze and see him jump. She noticed his Italian shoes, the trousers flawlessly creased, and glanced at her own faded Levis. But his hair. His hair was a jostled mess, tumbling across one eye. She knew she could love him for his hair alone.

"Wait!" she called, scrambling out of her seat and joining him in the doorway. "I want to paint you. I want to do your portrait."

"Really?"

She saw the golden light revisit his features. "Yes," she said. "Really. Really, truly."

"I'm flattered."

"Can I do it, then?"

"I've never had my portrait done before."

"It will be watercolor," she said. "I'll paint it with Venetian water."

"When?"

"Today?"

"Let's see," he said. "I could do it this afternoon. Where?"

"Do you know the *fondamenta* near where the Rio di San Toma meets the Grand Canal? It's across from the Palazzo Mocenigo —"

"Where Byron lived?" he asked.

"Exactly," she said. "With Byron's residence in the background."

He smiled into her eyes. "I'll be there at sixteen hundred hours."

She left the Hotel Accademia–Villa Maravegie feeling weightless, adoring the mercurial skies, the heaving winds and skidding light. She mentally ran through her inventory: paints, paper, brushes, sponges. He was right, of course. She should create her own visions. Suddenly the months of classes on restoration technology, on solvents, polyester resins, infrared and ultraviolet analyses, which had seemed so exciting, struck her as insignificant. Suddenly her father's well-reasoned arguments about the *business* of art seemed cowardly. She imagined the future restorationists who would someday resurrect her paintings.

A group of schoolgirls in green plaid skirts and white shirts piled up behind her on the tiny footbridge across to the Galerie dell' Accademia. *"Scusi, scusi,"* they said, giggling, squeezing past her one by one. Augusta slowed down so they could storm the museum ahead of her.

She found herself in Room X, in front of Tintoretto's *Re-*

moval of the Body of Saint Mark, depicting the first and most
famous of Venice's pious thefts: the robbery of the cadaver of
Saint Mark the Evangelist from the city of Alexandria. Augusta
studied the livid orange sky bursting with lightning, the vanishing geometry of white colonnaded buildings, the ghostly
spirits of infidel Egyptians fleeing in fear. Four righteous Venetians carried Saint Mark out of the city in their arms, his posture cruciform and yet, unlike Christ, earthbound, weighty,
and sallow.

At the Libraio a San Barnaba she spent an exorbitant sum
for an English-language version of *Don Juan.* From there she
walked to the Cartoleria Accademia for a new tube of bleu de
Saxe paint, a telescoping wooden easel from Germany, and a
tablet of huge, handmade watercolor paper. Throughout these
transactions she mentally composed the letter to her father
asking for money to cover her unforeseen expenses (the *business,* after all). Then, feeling guilty, she had only a caffè latte for
lunch, loading it with powdered chocolate for energy.

At three o'clock that afternoon the light performed one of
Venice's frequent minor miracles. Shafts of amber dropped
through the clouds to spear an onyx-black gondola on the
Grand Canal as Augusta scrambled to erect her new easel. She
sponged a sheet of paper with water and dug through the
tubes of paint in her box, mixing a palette of cyan blue and
burnt umber. Sweeping the color across the paper, she allowed
a few tendrils to bleed down as rain showers, then touched the
linings of the clouds with yellow ocher to make broken sunlight. Raw sienna mixed with Paris white became a wall of
dusty pink palazzi. The canal itself appeared, mirroring the
colors and shapes of the top half of the painting, only wetter
and darker. A gondola sped through, its iron *ferro* glinting sil-

ver, the fluttering red ribbon on the gondolier's straw hat setting the motion and focus for the whole picture.

When she was finished she heard Bedford de Banville-Hughes's voice behind her. "It's lovely, Augusta."

"Mr. de Banville-Hughes."

"You can call me Bedford."

"Thank you."

"You know," he said, pointing across the canal, "that the Palazzo Mocenigo is where Byron lived in 1818, along with a monkey, a wolf, a fox, and Margarita Cogni, a baker's wife who ran off to be with him and who later stabbed him with a fork and then threw herself into the canal. He wrote the first canto of *Don Juan* there."

"Wonderful," said Augusta, smiling. She led him to the top of a stone mooring block on the edge of the Grand Canal, trying to ignore the electric charges that seemed to move through her fingers. "I want to paint you holding your biography, here, with the Palazzo Mocenigo in the background. I thought you could be reading from your book. Which is how I'll paint you. But then I thought, you're likely to be bored while I sketch, so I brought you this." She handed him the English copy of *Don Juan.* "To read aloud from."

He flipped the pages. "How perfect. I'd love to."

Just as she'd hoped, the golden color came back into his face.

Returning to her easel, Augusta tore the gondola painting off the tablet and set it on her painting box to dry. "I'm only going to sketch today. I'll use this picture as an example of color, later, in my studio." She studied him to see if he noticed the small lie about her room.

"So you won't finish today?"

"No," she said, shaking her head, imagining the end of her

painting and the end of her relationship with de Banville-Hughes.

"Should I pose?" he asked, looking around self-consciously.

"I'll pose you. Get comfortable and then I'll move you."

He stood stiffly, legs together, book open at his waist. She studied the scene, tilting her head as she ran the damp bristles of a paintbrush through her fingers. "Let's see," she said. Climbing the mooring beside him, she took his chin in her hand and turned it to the right, feeling the resistance in his neck and the awkwardness in her own touch. "And down," she said, angling his head toward his shoulder. "And like this," she said, pulling his left shoulder back. She took his right arm, bent it at the elbow, and placed the book in his hand, then took his left arm and crossed it over his waist, the hand resting in the crook of the right elbow. She could feel him bend, and a thrill surged through her. "And now here," she said, stepping down, pulling on his left knee until the leg bent out. She walked back to her easel. The pose was graceful, and his long lines held it well. His profile stood in sharp relief against the pink palazzo across the canal.

"Okay," she said to herself, selecting a slender stick of charcoal from her painting box.

"Shall I read?" he asked.

She placed a gray test line on the white paper.

"I'll read from Canto the Second, when the young Don Juan has been saved from his shipwreck by the Greek beauty Haidée."

> There, breathless, with his digging nails he
> clung
> Fast to the sand —

Augusta studied the drape of his limbs, found the lines of motion, and organized them in her mind. De Banville-Hughes looked up from his reading, caught her studying him, and smiled.

"Are you comfortable?" she asked.

"Just fine," he said. "It seems fitting to be reading Byron aloud on the Grand Canal."

> *How long in his damp trance young Juan lay*
> *He knew not, for the earth was gone for him.*

Augusta refocused her eyes until the world in front of her melted into light and shadow. She noted the translucent glint of yellow through de Banville-Hughes's hair, the purple shadows sweeping down his cheek, and his long fingers flexing as he read.

> *And then once more his feelings back were brought,*
> *And slowly by his swimming eyes was seen*
> *A lovely female face of seventeen.*

Green light pulsed off the canal onto pink buildings, and she made a note to herself in the left margin of her paper: Guignet's green. Studying his shadow on the dull stone, she heard him ask, "Aren't you going to draw?"

"Drawing's the easy part." She smiled.

> *And in her air*
> *There was a something which bespoke command,*
> *As one who was a lady in the land.*

She let his words drift through her, no more conscious of them than of her own breath. Lifting the stick of charcoal, she made a long, light line and crossed it. Arms appeared. A horizon of shoulders. Legs. A neck arc. *It was such pleasure to behold him, such / Enlargement of existence to partake / Nature with him.* As the light fell, the colors reddened and the landscape shone. *Oil silk,* wrote Augusta in the left margin. *To thrill beneath his touch, / To watch him slumbering, and to see him wake.*

"Would you like to rest?" she asked. He smiled, shook his head. She heard a water taxi honk at a gondola and the gondolier shout back, *Cretino!* She heard a man and a woman behind her critique her work (or was it the view?) in German. Or was it Swedish? Four schoolboys with a soccer ball kicked their way past the mooring block. *To live with him forever were too much; / But then the thought of parting made her quake; / He was her own, her ocean-treasure, cast / Like a rich wreck — her first love, and her last.* A lone church bell rang, and the sinking sun cradled de Banville-Hughes. *Tenebroso,* thought Augusta, seeing in her mind's eye Caravaggio's paintings of dark and light and hearing in her mind the words that best described him: *darkness gave him light.*

The canal lamps blinked on in their wrought iron stands.

"Augusta," said de Banville-Hughes softly. "I can hardly see to read. How can you draw?"

She looked up. "I'm sorry. You must be tired."

"Hungry," he said, stepping down. "I'm famished."

She closed the tablet on her drawing.

"May I see it?"

"Of course," she said, "when it's finished." She collected her paints, brushes, put them away in the box, then closed up the easel and wiped her hands on a streaked rag.

"May I take you out to eat?" he asked, hoisting her painting box. She was pleased that she was not surprised at his offer, as she would have imagined earlier.

They joined the throngs of Venetians clattering down narrow streets past food merchants and their carts filled with tomatoes and bulbs of fennel. Augusta admired the way de Banville-Hughes eased gracefully past fat matrons with string shopping bags in hand and squeezed through the tiny, crowded *sotoportegos* under ancient buildings. She could see that the streets excited him.

He led her up a tiny alley beyond the crowds. They stood on an arched stone footbridge watching the last hint of Indian red seep from the sky and the water. In the distance, people hurried in silhouette over another bridge. "If you allow yourself," he said, "you can imagine this is the seventeenth century, that it's Carnival, and all these Venetians are masked, incognito, hurrying to eat and sing, gamble, and make love with forbidden partners inside rocking gondolas."

At an old-fashioned *bacaro* with an enormous wine list scribbled on a chalkboard on the wall, they edged their way through the crowds to the bar. De Banville-Hughes used eager but eccentric Italian to order a bottle of red Bardolino and an array of small *cichetti:* smoked mussels, pickled onions, artichoke hearts crisped in olive oil and rosemary. They poured the wine into tumblers and clicked them together. "To Venice," he said, "and all its beauties."

They drank glass after glass of wine, until Augusta felt her face flush and the roar in the room grew louder. Smoke feathered from dozens of cigarettes: tarry French, Indonesian clove, perfumed Turkish. A jukebox played arias, and patrons erratically sang along. Roving waiters carried stacks of small plates of food, which Augusta reached over and grabbed as they passed. They ate porcini mushroom polenta, sard in saor, grilled crabs granceola, spaghetti with garlic and chiles. They finished the Bardolino and drank a Refosco from Friuli.

De Banville-Hughes teased Augusta's memory for vignettes of home: fishing for crawdads on the Arkansas River, climbing so high into the copper beeches that the branches swayed under her weight. He began to describe his life at Trinity College but quickly sidetracked to Byron's life there: how Byron had been expelled for keeping a pet bear in his room and for skinny-dipping in the fountain of the Great Court.

They ordered sambuca with floating coffee beans and laughed and made toasts to each other's pasts. Then he reached for her hands beside the wax-covered rosé bottle that held a sputtering candle.

"Why did you write the name of your hotel in my book last night?" she asked.

He drew back.

"I'm just curious."

He smiled apologetically. *"For man, to man so oft unjust, / Is always so to women."* She saw a flicker of helplessness in his green eyes and found herself relishing it.

Later they strolled arm in arm through the Piazza San Marco, admiring the stars and the glittering gold domes across the lagoon. The square was filled with lovers and stray cats hunting for the night's rewards. A gondolier beckoned to them as a group of German tourists sang beer songs on the steps of the Palazzo Ducale.

She went back to his hotel with him and sank into the luxury of his room: the soft bed and expensive bedclothes, the down pillows with silk covers. He opened the tall windows to let the air in, and she took the moment to study his naked body in the light reflecting off the canal. Thin and patient, filled with the same passive expectation as his handshake. Yet despite his age — probably fifteen years older than she — there wasn't a mark anywhere on it: an empty canvas. When he came back to the bed, she took the skin on his chest between her teeth and bit down.

Later they listened to waves slap in the canal. "What would Byron have thought of us?" asked Augusta. He got up and felt in the dark for his books, and took one into the light near the open window. "This is what he wrote to a friend and critic of *Don Juan: Confess, confess — you dog and be candid . . . It may be bawdy but is it not good English? It may be profligate but is it not* life?"

The next morning Augusta went home to paint. She left de Banville-Hughes in the breakfast room, having made plans to meet at four o'clock. The sky outside was as clear as glass and cold. Lines of laundry strung above alleyways snapped on stiff winds. Flocks of swifts heeled around chimney pots and hurtled low over the canals, scraping gnats from the spray.

By the time she reached her flat she felt cleansed of the emotions of the previous day. When she cranked open the heavy wooden blinds on the outside of her windows, the light entered, and she erected her easel in the center of it, then set her color sketch of the Grand Canal and the charcoal sketch of de Banville-Hughes on the floor. She filled her drinking cup with water from the *bagno* down the hall and placed de Banville-Hughes's book on the windowsill. Stripping to her underpants, undershirt, and socks, she faced her easel, unencumbered. She soaked the sponge in the water glass and wet the paper. There: the painting was committed. Now she had to move.

She worked quickly. The sky came in like yesterday's, heavy, swollen, but redder, the clouds more active, with a shimmer of lightning. She found herself amending the perspective of the buildings on the Grand Canal until they faded to a vanishing point behind de Banville-Hughes. As she mixed pinks and pearl white, the buildings began to shimmer like ghosts against the roiling sky. This surprised her. Only on the waterline, nearest to the reflections in the canal, did the *palazzi* soak up color, like a blooming welt. She compared the painting with her color sketch of the day before and found that although it was not what she'd planned, it seemed authentic. She moved on.

Shifting her gaze to de Banville-Hughes's biography on her windowsill, she began to imagine how she would paint it in his hands. Luckily, *The Aphrodisia of a Romantic Poet: Lord Byron and the Impossible Passions of the Nineteenth Century* had a portrait of Byron's face on the cover, which would play nicely against de Banville-Hughes's profile. But even as her mind was thinking, her left hand was picking the charcoal stick from her painting box and adding a series of rapid strokes. She drew long lines of pathos, the drape of sorrow, then short lines to show something else: the excitement of adoration. She drew with confidence, then studied her efforts like a critic, struggling to see, to understand. What had she made?

Something radically different from what she'd intended. Nevertheless, she picked up her paintbrushes and mixed a luteous yellow with leek green and burnt sulfur. The newly sketched form took color, a rancid color she could almost smell. Turning to the figure of de Banville-Hughes, she mixed a palette of blowsy rose, pearl white, and Japanese lacquer red. In this version of yesterday's events, he perched nervously on the mooring block, midway between sky and water. His eyes glowed cobalt green, rimmed in black kohl. Augusta's head began to hurt as she added a black Carnival mask, brushed up onto his forehead, and a black Carnival cape that partly concealed his stockinged legs and high heels. She painted his face, powdered, colored, made up, with wet lips that smiled in delight at the prize in his arms: the corpse of Lord Byron, dead yellow, limp, draped in cruciform around de Banville-Hughes's legs. Then, before she could change her mind or give it any thought at all, Augusta picked up a Chinese calligraphy brush from her painting box, dipped it into a puddle of blue-black paint, and wrote the title words across the bottom of her picture: *The Biographer Stealing from the Dead.*

Retreating to the far side of her room as the painting dried, Augusta waited apprehensively. The picture was grotesque. Surely she could never show it to de Banville-Hughes. Turning away from it, she leaned out the window to watch an old woman tending pots of geraniums in the shade. A cat lay beside her. If Augusta painted this old woman poisoning weeds or the cat eating a bird, would it be any less true?

Wrapping her painting in brown paper, she set off for Vaporetto No. 1 and took a seat belowdecks, where she could watch the brown sea of the Grand Canal sluice over the windows. Row after row of slimy stone foundations swept past as bricked-in windows and doors half under water took the dirty slap from the vaporetto's wake. She tried to imagine Byron swimming for health in the canals but could think only of Margarita Cogni, the baker's wife, trying to kill herself.

He was waiting for her outside the Basilica di San Marco, on the Loggia dei Cavalli, the balcony on the façade with the famous *quadriga* of bronze chariot horses. She saw him at the far left, his back to her, studying the crowds in the plaza below and the rocketing flocks of pigeons. A light breeze lifted the edges of his tweed jacket and pulled at his hair. She felt an echo of affection, then sadness as she shifted her painting to the other arm and walked toward him.

"Bedford," she said.

"Augusta." He leaned down to kiss her. "Isn't it wonderful up here? Almost nobody ever makes it."

"Yes," she said, trying to smile as she saw him studying the wrapped paper under her arm.

"Have you seen the real horses?" he asked nervously.

She shook her head.

He took her by the hand and led her back inside to the nearly empty gallery with four bronze horses identical to the ones out on the loggia. "These are the real ones," he said, "the only four horses of a triumphal chariot from antiquity. But nobody knows which antiquity. They might be Greek, third century B.C., or Roman, second century A.D."

"I see," said Augusta.

"Constantine the Great stole them from whomever and took them to his new capital. The Venetians stole them from Constantinople —"

"They're beautiful," she said, walking around the sculpted haunches.

"Art, like ghosts, never rests," he said.

She turned to face him. "I've finished your portrait, Bedford."

"I see that. Shall we go outside and have a look?"

"It's not what I thought it would be," she said, following him back to the loggia. The sunlight struck a steel-blue shadow and he stopped, half inside it, leaning against the balustrade, waiting. "I mean, it turned into something I'd never imagined." His smile was warm. His hair tumbled in the breeze. "I considered not showing it to you."

"Is it good?" he asked.

She looked at him before answering, then nodded, acknowledging what she now believed to be the truth.

"That's all that matters," he said.

She tried unwrapping the brown paper, but the wind kept tossing it back across the picture. He leaned over, his back to her, lifted the painting free, and held it flat against the top of the balustrade.

"I'm sorry," she said as she saw him flinch.

"Is this what you see?" His voice was low, and he did not turn around. A pigeon clapped to rest on the head of a bronze horse.

"Only for a moment," she said. "I saw that just briefly."

A sound struggled from him as his hand crept toward his mouth. The pigeon cooed into the bronze horse's ear.

"I shouldn't have shown it to you," said Augusta.

"No."

"I'll take it back," she said, reaching.

His finger traced the yellow line of Byron's arm, his hand hovering over the black cape and stockinged leg.

"You can burn it if you want to," she said.

He laughed and the pigeon flew away.

Touching his hand, Augusta stroked his long fingers, turned the hand palm up, and kissed the pulse on the soft underside of his wrist.

Senti's Last Elephant

SENTI DOES NOT KNOW how to read. Neither Setswana, his native tongue, nor English, nor Fanagalo, all lingua francas here in Botswana. Not even Afrikaans, used by the white farm owners just over the border in South Africa. He can speak some of all these languages, but he can't read or write a word of any of them, a fact that embarrasses him when a tourist occasionally asks him to spell the word for, say, mopaneveld.

"Elephant-tree savanna," he translates, thereby avoiding the discomfort of his illiteracy.

A dying elephant writes its obituary in the earth. This Senti knows. It writes: *I am an ancient female whose teeth, the machinery of my digestion, are gone.* Or: *I am a young calf, less than a year old, and here my herd has stopped and surrounded me as I rest, awaiting the gathering of my strength so together we can continue on to the edge of the Limpopo River, to that bend where*

*the shade of the umbrella thorns preserves twin pools of water in
an otherwise dry bed.*

The elephant whose tracks Senti found this morning wrote
a shuffling and confused story in the dust around the Lalapanzi spring last night: *I am a bull in my prime who has been
dying now for some weeks, and although I am greatly weakened
and at times only barely conscious, I have become more dangerous than ever.*

Because of this, Senti decides to avoid the spring and swings
the LandCruiser around, stepping on the clutch and reaching
with his right arm across the steering wheel for the stick shift.
In the years since he lost his left arm he has learned to drive
as smoothly as he ever could with two arms, and now, back-
tracking through the belt of riparian forest along the edge of
the Majale River, he weaves expertly among massive mashatu
trees.

High overhead, pairs of woodland kingfishers as bright as
sapphires loose their descending duets with the obsessive mo-
notony of crickets: *yimp-trrrrrrr, yimp-trrrrrrrr*. His passengers, in the back, have no idea where he's going. Like all
foreigners, they seem unable to ground themselves in this
landscape, as old as human genesis itself.

The soil of Mashatu Game Reserve is an ancient, rusty red,
cooked down to its essential elements by the African sun, its
tiny particles scattered season after season by the rains as water
slowly equalizes the land, carrying hilltops and long-extinct
volcanoes down their own subsiding slopes to fill valleys and
riverbeds. Bit by bit the landscape turns itself inside out, revealing buried treasures of geodes, agates, quartz crystals, tri-
lobite fossils, nickel-shiny meteorites, and hundred-thousand-

year-old stone tools carefully chipped by those who might well have been Senti's ancestors.

He swings back by Main Camp, radioing in first so that Pretty from the kitchen can meet his passengers with cold glasses of lemonade. Senti walks over to John's hut, where the armory is stored under lock and key. John is waiting for him with the .458, a bolt-action elephant gun.

"Be careful," says John.

Senti nods.

Back at the LandCruiser, the guests — a stockbroker from Texas, his wife, his two daughters, and the wife's elderly mother — are chatting with Pretty, who wears the fire-engine-red dress and scarf favored by Batswanan women. Straight as a river reed she stands, the tray with three now empty glasses balanced on her head as she waits patiently for the daughters to finish their drinks. "*Dumela*," says Senti, flashing her a smile. She coyly dips a shoulder and lowers her eyes, all without affecting the delicate alignment of tray, neck, lemonade glasses, head.

He unclips the Czechoslovakian-made .375 rifle from the hood of the LandCruiser, places it across the empty passenger seat beside him, and hooks the barrel and butt of the .458 into its place.

"Want to come?" he teases Pretty in Setswana.

She swings an arm up and the tray slides from her head as fluidly as a bird taking off into the wind. Collecting the daughters' lemonade glasses, she turns her back to Senti, then glances over her shoulder at him before saying softly into the empty air ahead of her, "Some of us have work to do, man."

Senti starts the engine.

"That's quite a rifle," says the stockbroker from the back.

"Yes," says Senti, turning around, smiling. His job is to tend to the tourists and their questions regardless of any other matter at hand, except, of course, safety.

The wife and daughters focus their attention on the .458 clipped across the hood, and the stockbroker takes advantage of this sudden interest to assert his knowledge.

"Why a lion gun?" he asks.

During the three days Senti has spent with this family in the LandCruiser, they have been undergoing what is by now, to Senti, a familiar transformation. The husband (whose idea this trip was and who brought them all the way to Africa to show them what worlds his wealth could provide) is slowly losing face. Out here, far from Wall Street and surrounded by the terrific appetites and talents of lions, wildebeests, leopards, and elephants, his family is coming to see that their beloved and heretofore invincible patriarch is as vulnerable as any woman. As a result, they're beginning to recast their image of the male into something resembling Senti himself.

It's an uncomfortable reshuffling of hierarchy, especially inside such a small vehicle. Invariably the husband turns defensive. Sometimes he argues with Senti, or becomes overbearingly commanding, barking orders as if Senti were nothing more than a bush valet. Occasionally the husband excuses himself from the game drives altogether (as the stockbroker did yesterday), remaining behind at the lodge to fortify himself with the familiar, shouting business directives via the radio to underlings at home.

Yet Senti is glad to have him back today. He knows this trip will not be successful in the family's memory unless they can put to rest their conflicts in the LandCruiser. But he also needs to answer truthfully about the gun.

"No," he says, turning again to smile. "This is not a lion gun but an elephant gun."

The husband and wife are sitting directly behind him in the open back of the LandCruiser, the daughters and grandmother one row farther back. Mokabela, the tracker, perches on the jumpseat at the rear.

"You could use it to shoot lions though, right?" says the husband, readjusting his baseball cap.

"Of course," says Senti, trying to mollify him.

But he can see the doubt in the women's eyes.

"I think he means, honey," says the wife, "that he'd really use the other gun to shoot lions."

"Why would you want to shoot any of them?" says the elder daughter, a sixteen-year-old who celebrated her birthday here the day before yesterday. Because of this trip to Africa, she has decided to become a biologist when she grows up. Senti knows this because the family teases her about the fact that during their last vacation, to Italy, she decided to be an archaeologist, and before that, an astronaut.

"Yes, that's right," says Senti. "We don't want to shoot anything."

He smiles. The women smile. The grandmother adjusts her hearing aid. Senti turns forward, ready to drive on.

"What did he say?" asks the grandmother as Senti swivels back again.

"He said we're not going to shoot anything," says the younger daughter, who looks enough like the mother for Senti to understand exactly what makeup accomplishes, or rather what it will accomplish for her in a few years' time.

The husband doesn't smile. "When I'm out deer hunting," he says, "I prefer to know I have something with me that will cope with bears or cougars as well."

"Don't be barbaric, Daddy," says the elder daughter.

"We are what we are because we're hunters," says the father. "Isn't that so, Senti?"

"You've been hunting, like, three times in your entire life," says the younger daughter.

"When I was a boy —" starts the father.

"And you never actually killed anything," interrupts the elder daughter.

"Face it, Daddy," says the younger daughter. "You're just a weekend warrior."

"Darling!" The mother laughs, looking at Senti with her beautiful smile. "Where do you learn such things?"

"I'll tell you where the real hunting goes on these days," says the father, warming up for what seems to be a too-familiar lecture.

"We *know!*" shout the daughters.

"*You* wouldn't know this, though, Senti," says the father, trying to make eye contact. But Senti is distracted by the sight of Pretty sauntering up to John outside the reception hut, her eyes still downcast, yet a kind of sullen coquettishness evident in the sway of her hips. They're too far away for him to hear what's being said, but she glances Senti's way when John isn't looking. Senti smiles back, but not too strongly. Just with one side of his mouth. He knows you don't win women with overeagerness. You work downwind, so to speak.

The guests are staring at him expectantly, and he realizes he has missed something. A question.

"Pardon me?" he says.

"I said," says the father, "that isn't it true that if we hadn't become hunters, we'd still be like these baboons, picking seeds off the ground."

Senti thinks it was probably a good line when he said it the first time, as it brought this argumentative family to a stop. But it has lost some power in the retelling.

"What's wrong with baboons?" says the younger daughter. "I love baboons."

"Baboons," says Senti, carefully addressing the daughter, "are very good hunters. In the Limpopo they catch fish. They take springhares from their holes in the ground. On the farms here they steal baby sheep and goats."

"Honey," says the wife, playfully punching the husband's shoulder, "I think you'd better stick to price-earnings ratios."

Affection tempers her sarcasm, and the others laugh gently. Senti turns forward again, relieved to be absolved from the husband's real question.

A healthy elephant writes a beautiful cursive. The prints of the rounded front feet, bigger than dinner plates, are partially erased by the sweep of the back legs trailing lazily through the earth. In a herd of females, the last will leave her signature on top of the others, though traces of the forerunners remain: the small footprint of an infant, or the sinuous drag-mark of a trunk as an elephant inhales dust and sprays it up over her ears to drive off tsetses. The dust, falling like rain, leaves tiny craters on the ground.

Senti's father taught him all this, and more. Together they tracked in the bush, Father squatting beside the trail, patiently pointing with the tip of a small twig so Senti could learn to read the words written in the earth in their correct syntax.

"Here is the female with no tusks," Father would say, recognizing the elephant by the split heel of a rear foot. "And here," he added, pointing to a set of small tracks with a characteristic W shape, "the genet walked by later last night." Tracing a spidery path right up to the insect's newly built lair, he continued, "And here, you see, the ant lion left his own trail on top of both first thing this morning."

Driving out of Main Camp, Senti heads north, away from Lalapanzi spring. Which is the best he can do at the moment, knowing full well that a dying elephant, especially male and alone, is intrinsically unpredictable in its behavior. Short of tracking it, which is far too dangerous with tourists aboard, he can try only to stay beyond the range it has likely covered since last night.

"*Thutlwa*," says Mokabela, the tracker.

"Giraffe," says Senti, pointing.

He slows the LandCruiser so the daughters can take snapshots. Out here in Mashatu the giraffes are much taller than the bush itself. Elephants keep the mopaneveld trimmed to a comfortable height for them, but it forces the giraffes to eat with their necks perpetually bent. Worse, the giraffes are living lightning rods, and many a thunderstorm leaves one struck down and splayed across the landscape like a giant, five-limbed, spotted star.

"*Phala*," says Mokabela from the back.

A tiny female bounds off the track far ahead of them. It's unusual for an impala to be alone, but as this is the birthing season, Senti slows the vehicle, knowing what to expect. Just off the trail lies a perfectly formed impala baby, born only a moment before, now dead.

"Stillborn," says Senti, surprised.

Its cinnamon-colored coat is soft and wet, the large eyes unopened, back legs tucked into a fetal curl, front legs raised together over its head as if it were diving headfirst out of the womb. Senti engages the handbrake and steps down from the LandCruiser.

"It's still warm," he says.

Mokabela grunts, lifts his chin.

"What did he say?" asks the wife.

"He says now it will be food for the jackals."

"Can we get out?" asks the elder daughter.

"Sorry," he says. "But remember, you must stay inside at all times, unless we're out in the open." He glances up at the passengers as they study the dead impala. The daughters and grandmother look sad, the wife excited, almost aggressive. He has caught that expression on her face before. The husband? He's not sure. Bored, perhaps. Senti resolves to find him something of interest. Lion. Or, if they're lucky, cheetah.

The soil of Mashatu is the red, oxidized remains of ancient lava, imprintable in both the dry and the wet season. Lions particularly like to walk along the LandCruiser tracks, and patrol them as regularly as the vehicles themselves do, their six-inch pugmarks weaving over the treadmarks in a lightfooted waltz. The trail Senti is driving now, up the bed of the Jwala River, is the current boundary marker between two warring prides, the Jwala pride to the north and the Motloutses to the south. The sandy river, dry, twisting, and narrow, is cluttered with lion spoor.

The Jwalas, composed of a rare coalition of five adult males — brothers in their prime at eight years old, each beautifully outfitted in a mixed blond-and-black mane — are astonishingly successful at the moment. The Motloutse pride is an up-and-coming mixture of three four-and-a-half-year-old brothers and one six-year-old outsider, who came in over the border from Zimbabwe. Senti has watched this loner slowly affiliating himself with the Motloutses for the past seven months, acting with great reserve and diplomacy, staying at a distance, always greeting the pride with peaceful puffing calls, *pfff-pfff, pfff-pfff,* generously abandoning his kills to them, and then, tentatively, beginning to hunt beside them. With great restraint, he has avoided any sexual contact with the females. All within the pride know that someday soon he and the three brothers will leave this territory and take on the Jwalas, or a pride to the west, in the Kalahari.

The elder daughter decides that she wants to study the big cats after hearing all this.

"It's a lion soap opera," says the mother.

The dry ravine, lined with tamboti trees and huge, beautiful specimens of mashatus, is acrid with the smell of lion urine. Each pride makes forays down here when it is sure that the other is away and sprays everything in sight.

Mokabela points up the gully through thick bush.

Senti turns the wheel and engages the four-wheel drive, and the LandCruiser climbs the nearly vertical bluff with the tenacity of a tank, its reinforced front end knocking down and running over a thicket of stinky-shepherd trees, which release their carrion stench in an eye-watering burst.

"Phew," says the younger daughter.

"Is something dead?" asks the mother.

Something is always dead, thinks Senti, but he turns his head and says over his shoulder, "No. Just these trees smell dead."

"Isn't that strange, honey?" says the wife to her husband.

"What?"

"That trees would smell dead?"

"What's so strange about that?"

The husband, Senti recognizes, is refusing to show any surprise, as that would acknowledge ignorance.

"You never smelled trees that smelled dead before, Daddy," says the younger daughter.

"I don't smell anything," says the grandmother.

"Me neither," says the husband, laughing playfully, so they know he's lying.

Flocks of green-spotted doves flush from the ground ahead of them, then alight in the trees behind, cooing in the soft and melodic percussion of the bush, *du-du . . . du-du . . . du-du-dudu-du-du-du.*

Senti's father was a tracker, first for white hunters, later for poaching conglomerates headquartered in Johannesburg and then, during the apartheid blockade, in Harare. Like Senti, he grew up in this landscape known as the Tuli Block and was familiar with every sandstone massif, each belt of mopane forest, all the granite hills, and the rivers in every season, every mood.

When Senti was five years old, Father began taking him into the bush, teaching him the skills with which he would make his living. First the obvious: the twenty or thirty rhino middens maintained by each territorial male, huge dung piles advertising, as Father said, the strength of his gut. Then the subtle: the peculiar shitlike smell of the leopard's two-day-old catch, a tiny steenbok dangling incongruously high overhead in the pale foliage of the apple-leaf tree, its head draped upside down and its legs arched awkwardly backward, displaying the open body cavity. The smell, Father pointed out, was not of the carcass itself but of the heart, which the cat had buried in the leaf litter below.

Elephants were both the easiest and the most dangerous to track. Easy because of their noisy lifestyle, ripping away bark with tusks and trunks, knocking down fruiting trees, constantly trumpeting to each other, or rumbling, or belching. But they were dangerous in those days before the establishment of the game reserve (when warfare raged between elephants and men), because if they found you, they charged.

Although some poachers used machine guns, Senti and his father could afford only rifles and were therefore reduced to one carefully placed shot each. They could shoot nearly anywhere, even in the head, even with a .458, but an enraged elephant could survive sometimes for weeks. To kill, they needed to sever the spine. Up at the occiput was best. Senti learned this, along with the lesson that he should outwait his excitement, or impatience, or whatever it was that made his trigger finger itch, until near-boredom assured a good shot. He should also, Father said, shoot the biggest elephant first, the matriarch, because even after her skull was stripped of its ivory her family would return to fondle the bones. From a young age this bothered Senti, the way time and again he and his father took advantage of the elephants' grief to ambush the rest of the herd.

"Look at all those bones," says the elder daughter as Senti drives them off-track into open bush, through a carpet of dwarf yellow wildflowers raised by early storms. As always, he is surprised that it has taken three days for the first family member to notice Mashatu's bones, the lost vertebrae, detached occipitals, femurs, antlers, and ilia that decorate the red soils and yellow flowers like weatherworn pearls.

"That was a wildebeest killed by lion in 1996," says Senti.

"Really?" says the mother.

"Wow," says the elder daughter. "You remember that?"

Senti knows every bone here, to whom it belonged in life and who consumed its flesh in death. Only the largest bones survive the crushing skills of the hyenas, and the absolutely largest, the elephant skulls, become enduring landmarks by which the rangers radio interesting finds to each other, as in "A pair of bat-eared foxes is resting by the elephant skull on the Braaikoppie."

Mokabela points to the right.

Senti turns the wheel and they head into thicker mopane bush. He can smell it now.

"Tau," says Mokabela.

Senti turns off the engine. In the sudden quiet, sound becomes as bright and layered as a rainbow: the humming of nursing cubs, the crunching of bones, the rasp of a cat tongue licking flesh away.

"There are lion here," says Senti, very quietly.

"Cool," says the younger daughter.

"They are eating something now," says Senti. "Can you see? Through there. A zebra."

"I can't see anything," says the mother.

"I see," says the husband.

"No, not there," says Senti, pointing. "Just through there."

Senti, who can smell the lioness's milk, knows from the tracks they've been following for the last hour that this is the female with four cubs, along with her own pregnant mother. Two of the four adult women of the Motloutse pride.

He starts up the engine again and circles around to the left.

"Hey, right there," says the father.

Senti cuts the engine. Fifteen feet away lies the mother,

suckling two of the cubs. The others play tug-of-war with a blood-red rib bone. The grandmother lioness is the one making the rasping sounds as she cleans tendons and ligaments from a severed front leg. Behind them, perhaps another twenty feet away, lies the dead zebra, opened and excavated from belly to chest. A haze of flies adds its own sound.

"Just look at that," says the wife. "Can you believe it?"

"This is what we came for," says the husband.

"Africa," says the wife. "Isn't it incredible?"

The rib, in the jaws of one cub, twirls in the air.

"It's kind of gross," says the younger daughter.

The cub detaches itself from the bone to investigate the grandmother's switching tail. Without breaking the rhythm of her licking, the lioness growls, a sound low and percussive enough to rumble human bones.

"It's Darwinian," says the elder daughter.

"What's that mean?" asks her sister.

"It means it isn't good or bad, stupid. It just is."

In the distance Senti sees a pair of jackals, waiting.

"Is it safe," whispers the grandmother, leaning forward, "for that zebra to be so close to those lions?"

There's a moment of silence before the family bursts into laughter, causing the lioness to give a startled *woof* and fix her eyes on Senti. He starts the engine, knowing that of all things, lions don't like laughter: hyena words.

"Jesus, Nan," says the husband, crying tears of mirth. "That zebra is completely dead."

For eighteen years Senti worked with his father. Bone by bone, fascia by muscle, nerve by artery, the landscape assembled itself in his mind into a living anatomy containing many smaller working parts: the elephants, the baobab trees, the warthogs, the salt pans. In the beginning he believed that he and his father were simply two more aspects of this corpus. But as the years went by, as their life's work accumulated across the landscape in the form of hacked-up rhinoceros and elephant skulls, Senti's notion began to change. Eventually he and his father seemed less a part of the anatomy of the land than an outside force.

As his bush knowledge deepened, so did his qualms, until Senti began to believe he had filled up and exceeded his life's quotient of death, a feeling that weighed upon him. One fateful day the gravity of this notion pressed him down to the ground, to a place where he was relieved of the weight of it. Lightened, as it were, by one arm.

At the rock crossing on the Matabole River, not far from Main Camp, Senti slows the LandCruiser, then backs it up, following fresh spoor in the sand. This signature is unmistakable. Gone is the graceful rhythm of the stride. Like an elephant drunk on fermenting calabash fruit, this bull staggers and sometimes nearly falls. It's a script Senti knows well. As he also knows that this dying elephant will now remain by the water to drink and drink, trying to still the unquenchable thirst that accompanies the final failure of the kidneys.

Mokabela whistles softly.

"Yes," says Senti in Setswana, "he's nearby now."

A pool of water in the riverbed trickles slowly downstream to another pool, where a pair of saddle-billed storks are wading, trying to tempt fish to the lures of their pink feet and pink knees.

Senti speaks quietly into his headset, in Setswana so the

tourists won't understand, alerting the other rangers to the news. John, out searching, comes back to him on the radio, concerned that the elephant is too close to Main Camp, where the other guests, returning for breakfast, might well hear a gunshot.

Senti drives upriver in order to cross again near the eagle's nest. From the far bank he hears an elephant rumbling, the sound building into a growl, then a roar.

"Elephants," says the husband.

"Yes," says Senti. "They are coming down to the river to drink."

From behind a picturesque screen of flowering flame trees comes a herd of females, the matriarch bringing up the rear, slowed by the unsteady pace of a newborn calf traveling between her legs. The elephants pause, trunks twirling, sensing the LandCruiser.

"They don't see well," says Senti. "They are trying to hear us, and smell us."

The newborn flaps one ear nervously, the other ear still molded into a fetal fit alongside its head. An adult female advances to the water with both ears open to catch the wind. She dips her trunk, siphons the water, then relays it to her mouth. Others follow. Their smell drifts over to the LandCruiser, as warm and comforting as a barn.

"Isn't this wonderful, girls?" whispers the mother.

Low rumbles echo from the herd, companionable and peaceful.

"I like elephants the best," says the younger daughter.

The newborn reaches an unsteady trunk into the mouth of its mother, tasting the water she drinks.

"Where are their tusks?" asks the husband.

"Most don't have tusks now," says Senti.

"Why not?" asks the wife.

"Before," says Senti, "there were many poachers here. Now the elephants don't grow much ivory."

"Don't they need tusks?" asks the wife.

"Yes," says Senti. "Tusks are very useful."

"Some of them have one tusk," observes the younger daughter.

"You mean they're *evolving* without tusks?" asks the elder daughter.

Senti is not sure exactly what she means. "The hunters," he says, "took all the ivory. The only ones left are those who had little, or none. Their children grew up like them."

"That's natural selection," says the elder daughter.

"I'm not sure it's all that natural, honey," says the mother.

The newborn elephant bends down on its knees to drink with its mouth.

"You see how he is too small to use his trunk," says Senti.

"I say it's the Lord's will," says the grandmother.

"What?" says the mother.

"That the poor elephants have lost their tusks."

"Oh, lordy, lordy," teases the husband.

Senti turns to look the grandmother in the eye, and they share a smile.

"He *does* save elephants," she says, "as well as all us sinners."

Senti nods. The old woman alone must sense something of his past.

If his father had doubts about their work, Senti never knew it. At times he wished to discuss his own misgivings, but what were their options? They lived in a chasm of poverty, as dry and unyielding as drought. Worse, they were beholden to bosses, who in turn were beholden to other higher-ups, link by link across the landscape like the elephant fences erected by farmers in the region. Obligations enclosed Senti and prevented him from completing what he came to believe was his own natural migration, away from all the killing.

He hadn't shot well for a long time, which was an embarrassment to him, although his father, his eyesight failing from years in the sun, was unaware of or at least silent about Senti's mistakes. With their income dropping, the family began to go hungry, and the women, his father's three wives and their daughters, were driven to scavenging maize from neighboring white farms, where they risked being shot along with the marauding wildlife. Still Senti couldn't bring himself to improve his efforts. He hesitated. He made too much noise. He let the wind give him away. To add to their troubles, elephants were becoming scarce, and no one had seen a rhino here in three years. Some poachers were drifting to Johannesburg in search of other work, some toward the diamond mines in Namibia.

Occasionally Senti tracked false spoor down toward Solomon's Wall, the rock outcropping at the confluence of the Limpopo and the Motloutse, where even in the dry season deep pools of water offered the solace of reflection. There he and his father would perch on their haunches in the dappled shade beneath fever trees, Father napping, Senti swatting at flies and observing the aerial antics of carmine bee-eaters as they swooped down and punctured the stillness of the water.

One breezy afternoon in the dry season an elephant appeared from behind the rocks, surprising both itself and Senti. All hesitated, Senti to grab his rifle, the elephant to charge or withdraw, Father to awaken. Following that instant of stalemate, Senti looked away, allowing the elephant a safe retreat.

Then, in a blur, a sudden gallop of speed, the ground shaking, a furious scream, first elephant, then man, as Senti was knocked over and trampled under an enormous weight. He heard the cough of a .458 discharging, badly placed. Abandoning Senti, the elephant turned to punish Father, stomping, screaming, and tossing him into the water, where brain matter spilled out of his skull. From his ant's-eye view on the ground, Senti saw the elephant turn again and felt the vibration of the big feet slamming into the earth. Feebly, raising his uninjured arm to shield himself, Senti observed the elephant thunder up to him and then pass over, the dust rising in its wake.

Mokabela coughs, and Senti turns to look.

All the elephants have stopped drinking, ears raised. A network of blood vessels is visible through the thin parchment. Stretching one front leg forward, the matriarch rocks her foot back and forth in a threat display. A young female reaches out a trunk and pulls the newborn calf back from the water's edge and hurries it under her belly.

Senti starts the engine and eases the LandCruiser into reverse.

Mokabela points.

Behind them, leaning against a small tree in a mopane thicket, is the bull elephant they've been trying to avoid. He is as emaciated as a corpse, the contours of his skull rising sharply through his skin like those of the aged elephants that die in the dry season. But Senti can tell by the color of his ivory that he's not old at all, although his trunk droops listlessly on the ground and the nipples between his front legs protrude like the breasts of a nursing female. One leg is raised into the air, swaying there, as if he has momentarily forgotten where the ground lies. The mopane tree cracks under his weight, and he lurches forward onto the raised leg without lowering it and ends up twirling to the right and buckling onto his knees. As he falls away from the tree, Senti sees the bullet hole in his side, just behind the ribs, the wound white with maggots.

"Oh, my God," says the wife.

Ahead of them are elephants. Behind them lies the dying elephant, his head now resting on his single tusk. To either side lies the river, too deep to cross.

Senti speaks rapidly into the headset.

"What's wrong with that elephant?" says the younger daughter, watching the bull trying to leverage himself with tusk and trunk and succeeding only in plowing backward through the dry earth toward the LandCruiser.

"That's one sick elephant," says the husband.

Senti is calculating. How to drive around behind the bull? He'll have to drive straight through a thick stand of mopane, knocking it down.

"Mom, I don't like this anymore," says the younger daughter.

"Tlou," says Mokabela.

Senti glances forward. The herd of females across the river is advancing through the water toward the bull. They will want to raise him, Senti knows, even though without much ivory between them, it will be difficult.

"Uh-oh," says the wife.

The bull groans, a sound of pain and frustration.

The matriarch shakes her head back and forth, and her ears slap against her face. Another female rolls her trunk to her forehead, then unfurls it with a blast of air.

"Okay," says the husband. "I think they want us out of here."

But the back of the LandCruiser is not reinforced. In order

to drive over the mopane thicket, Senti needs to turn the vehicle around. He begins advancing and retreating, awkward with his one arm, juggling the stick shift, the steering wheel, trying with quick jerks to change direction.

"*Tau*," says Mokabela quietly.

Sure enough, padding through the trees that Senti would like to drive over, their footsteps as quiet as clouds, are four of the five brothers of the Jwala pride, yellow eyes fixed on the bull elephant.

Senti thinks, *So this is what the females heard.*

All four lions drop to a crouch, their ears flat. They are not afraid of the LandCruiser, as for many years now it has been a nearly constant and always neutral observer of their hunts.

"*Can* we get out of here?" asks the husband.

Senti would like to take one rifle or the other and hand it back to Mokabela in the rear, but he is fearful of the animals' response to the sight of it.

The elephants advance shoulder to shoulder, heads tossing, tails out, roaring. The lions fan out in a semicircle. Suddenly one springs forward and clamps onto the tip of the bull elephant's trunk, lying outstretched on the ground.

The bull screams. Or perhaps it's the girls in the back. Senti is not sure. The elephant lurches backward, dragging the lion with it. Senti feels the familiar thunder of the other elephants, now running. Realizing that he has turned the LandCruiser enough to charge toward the trees, he fights to straighten the wheel, only to see the husband reaching into the passenger seat for the .375.

Senti tries to grab it away from him but fails.

The husband levels the rifle over his wife's head.

"Daddy!" screams a daughter.

A lion turns their way. Senti floors the accelerator, and the vehicle leaps forward just as the cat jumps into it. Only his front legs make a purchase on the doorsill. Senti brakes hard, then accelerates, trying to dislodge him. The lion swats. A shot is fired. The lion drops away. Senti drives straight toward one of the other brothers crouching between him and the trees, forcing him to his feet with a surprised look on his face. From the seats behind him there's screaming and crying. Senti doesn't have time to look as he crashes into the thicket, grinding the trees under the chassis, where the smells of sap and death mingle.

He clears the thicket, feels the tires dig in and the Land-Cruiser accelerate rapidly.

"Is everyone all right back there?" he shouts.

Mokabela yells something he can't understand.

Senti keeps driving until they reach the open ground of an old salt pan, then slows the vehicle to glance behind him. Blood is everywhere. The girls are crying hysterically. Mokabela is trying to climb over them, past the grandmother, whose hands are around the mother's neck. He's trying to reach the source of the blood, somewhere in the seat behind Senti, coming from the husband, whose bloody hands cover the lower half of his face as he stares at his wife beside him. Her head has fallen back onto the reinforced clutch bar, and she is staring up at the sun. Senti sees blood pumping from between the grandmother's fingers as the wife blinks once, slowly. He takes the vehicle out of gear, sets the handbrake, and leaps into the seat behind him, forcing the husband out of the LandCruiser.

"Mommy!" shouts a daughter.

Senti brushes the grandmother's hands away from the wife's neck and sees where the bullet has torn her throat away.

The husband stands beside the vehicle, staring at his hands in puzzlement. Several fingers are missing, taken by the lion as It went after the rifle. His nose is split back from his face and lies against one cheek, held on by a flap of skin only. Mokabela is making him sit on the ground and is trying to push his nose back into place.

Despite the sobbing and the grandmother's loud prayers, Senti can still hear the other fight, the snarling of cats and the screaming of elephants. Looking up from where his hand presses against the wife's neck, trying to stem the blood, he sees a Jeep.

John pulls alongside, takes one look, and barks at Senti, "Get the man back in the vehicle."

"But the blood —"

"*Inside,*" snarls John.

Senti sees there isn't much blood left anyway, though the wife is still alive. Senti helps the husband into the passenger seat next to John, who takes the wheel as Mokabela jumps in beside the wife, and they speed away.

Alone, covered in blood, Senti stands by John's Jeep, staring at the dirt with its chaotic record of hiking boots, Senti's army boots, and Mokabela's sandals, punctuated by blood. He glances back across the salt pan toward the fight and sees that the lions have moved off but have not given up. Stepping wearily into the driver's seat, he engages the clutch. Three of the female elephants are jockeying for position, trying to raise the bull, but their tusks are too small. The other elephants are agitated, charging erratically toward the lions. Senti sees that half the bull's trunk is gone, chewed off by the cats, who now lie on their haunches in the shade to wait. Stopping the vehicle,

Senti unclips John's .458 and steps out. Crouching, he hefts the heavy rifle to his shoulder with his arm and braces it across the hood. His body is shaking, and it's difficult to get a sight through all the frenzy. But he's patient, there on his knees, prepared to wait as long as it takes for that feeling of peace to come upon him, the calm that precedes the one right shot.

The Dreams of Dogs

GRACE MAY SEEM an awkward name for an old woman with unkempt white hair that she cuts herself, erratically and idiosyncratically, with dog shears. The sparse dentition and the white whiskers on her upper lip, which she fingers frequently with arthritic hands, may also appear counterindicative of the name. But there are many meanings of the word, as Grace knows. She keeps the two volumes of the *Concise Oxford English Dictionary* on a wooden pulpit in the outhouse, because she feels the dictionary is a kind of prune juice for the mind.

Later in the day, when she taxes her body with physical labor, words pour forth, old words dredged up from their oblivion in the *OED* and brought back to life. This oratory relieves the congestion of her mind and lightens the hearts of her dogs, who dance alongside her as she shovels and saws and hammers. When she pauses to rest, the dogs, particularly Goliath, nuzzle her with warm snouts, inhaling her scent.

Grace has a vision that keeps her fit and will sustain her for many more years, past geriatrics and into centenarianism if need be. Only when she dies will all her labors come at last to fruition, although it will be a sorrowing crop, like the berries of the fat Solomon's seal that grow here, bitter and cathartic.

Grace's vision came to her many years ago, when she was a young woman with an inheritance and a broken heart. She bought two thousand acres embracing the entire spectrum of habitats within the Coast Range: deep redwood forests in the ravines, mixed stands of California bay and big-leaf maples at their upper margins, open oak woodlands on the rounded shoulders of the hills, and above it all, sun-baked chaparral. It would take Grace a lifetime to describe all that quickens and begets life on her property.

When she arrived from San Francisco in the early 1930s, she was alone except for one dog, a black German shepherd named Salvator. They were mourning the unexpected turn of events three months earlier that had widowed Grace at such a young age and left Salvator without a master. Grace was uncertain what to do with her land in the beginning. She and Salvator paced it, up and down, high and low, following foot trails and deer trails and forging their own trails to places where cottonwoods shaded the Navarro River and salmonberries ripened in late summer.

The first autumn, three Pomo women in castoff Salvation Army clothing knocked on Grace's door and politely asked if she would object to their collecting some of the leaves of the soap plant, the wild lily growing in open glens whose flowers unfurl only after sunset or in the fog.

"We have been collecting for many generations on this land," said a young woman shyly.

The ancient woman beside her said something in a language Grace had never heard before, and the young woman listened closely but said nothing more.

Grace admired their faces, broad and friendly, and their bare feet, broad and trail-friendly. "Please," she said, "come any time at all. Collect whatever you need, whatever you want."

After that, whenever the Pomo came to visit or collect or sit out by the river weaving baskets, Grace found herself relaxing. Once when she and Salvator wandered down to the river to ask what the words of a song they were singing meant, the old woman with a face as wrinkled as an apple twice overwintered in the root cellar answered in her bright, watery language.

"Far-Seeing Woman says do not worry about the future, white woman," said Marie.

"Is that all she said?" asked Grace.

"She spoke of the past," said Marie, smiling.

"What of the past?"

But Marie wouldn't say, and Far-Seeing Woman, noticing that Grace was still waiting, took Grace's hand and slapped the palm lightly with her own, in time to the music she was singing.

That first winter it rained and rained, powerful storms that swept in from the Pacific, bending limber trees under the wind and toppling old redwoods that fell not to the ground but only into the arms of neighbor trees, where they would continue to live, partially uprooted, for centuries more. The rain came so hard that some of the hills liquefied, slumping and sliding into avalanches of mud that swept down the canyons to dam the creeks. Grace was frightened at times and found herself questioning the decision that had brought her here, so far from the city. Friends in San Francisco who corresponded by mail sensed her doubt and tried to convince her to come back home.

But whenever Grace wavered, there was Salvator. The two of them huddled inside the old cabin by the woodstove, listening to the shingles flap on the roof, watching the dirt road that led out of the property gather its own water. Salvator slept on a large pillow that Grace sewed from a wool blanket and stuffed with bay leaves, as the Pomo advised her, to keep the fleas away. Later many dogs slept together in companionable piles on the bay-leaf pillows that Grace kept sewing and stuffing. But that first winter it was only Salvator, waking occasionally to glance at Grace as she sipped tea, checking in with drowsy eyes before dropping back into slumber and dreams, feet twitching, lips curling, whimpering. The dog's sorrows seemed very real to Grace.

It became clear that out here, so far from the home Grace and Salvator had shared with Samuel, the two needed something to fix their memories on. One winter morning, to Salvator's surprise, Grace cooked them both a thick oat porridge with butter, brown sugar, and raisins, then dressed herself in a pair of her husband's old trousers cinched around the waist with a belt and shooed Salvator ahead of her out of the house.

The dog paused at the threshold to sniff the unwelcoming air and the skies heavy with unshed rain.

Come, said Grace, grabbing the axe as they passed by the woodpile on their way up a westerly trail, through heavy clay mud that stuck to their feet and kicked up off their heels, splattering onto naked stands of California buckeye.

They climbed to the top of a high hill, from where in one direction they could see the rolling ridges of the Coast Range fading into mists out by the sea, and in the other the little valley with the red cabin far below, smoke stuttering from the chimney pipe.

Samuel had loved trees, and he had loved rocks. Here on this hilltop stood wind-stunted madrones and manzanitas, and a crag of green serpentinite mixed with blueschist, where in summer, Grace was sure, lizards would come out to sun and mountain lions with full bellies would stretch out before dawn. She walked round and round the crag, testing the views from all angles, while Salvator nosed the cracks in the rock, tail wagging, on the scent of mice.

Here we are, then, said Grace, taking the axe and starting to work.

Later that winter she hired a lumberman from Yorkville to take down an old madrone she chose for its trunk, which twisted and turned in graceful curlicues as it sought out sunlight in a dense forest. At Grace's direction, and against his own instincts, the man hand-planed the tree into six-foot-long boards, maintaining a wavy S-pattern in the planks. He tried hard to persuade Grace to use a straight section of the trunk, which would, he said, give her useful lumber. But Grace watched his initial disapproval of her idea develop into something close to intrigue and then appreciation as he worked with the tree. When he was finished, he brought his mule around to carry the planks up to the top of the hill with the rocky crag, where Grace would assemble them. "Good spot," he said, his own kind of left-handed compliment, before leading the mule back down.

From those boards Grace built her memorial, beautiful in

her eyes because of the fine grain of the wood and the way the planks curved around. Just as she'd pictured it in her mind, the pieces came together into a bench or, more accurately, a loveseat, the kind that was old-fashioned even then, with the two seats facing in opposite directions but sharing a common S-shaped back, so that two people sitting there would see each other while admiring different views.

The storms ended, but winter did not. A cold tule fog settled in the valley, making it hard for the smoke to rise from Grace's stovepipe in the morning. She had to prime the chimney by burning paper, which she didn't have much of, or kindling, which she had as much of as she was willing to split. The fog did peculiar things to sounds, dampening noises close by while bringing in those from far away and delivering them loudly and unexpectedly to Grace's home.

After the rains ended, Grace heard coyotes. At first just a lone howl, so low-pitched that she wondered if it was a wolf, but followed quickly by a chattering series of laughs and yodels, yelps, yips, and *I-eees:* the unmistakable sound of coyote song. It made Salvator wild, setting her ruff on edge and her eyes rolling until she burst out in her own singsong version.

Oddly enough, the coyotes relieved Grace's fears, although her friends from the city were horrified and begged her to come back to civilization. But Grace felt that the coyotes graced her land, their tracks in the mud and their scat on hilltops and at trail crossings telling of buoyant and confident rambles. These neighborly signs helped her feel at home.

They visited Samuel's memorial often, making the hard climb in silence, noting the subtle precursors of spring: the first shoots of the mission bells, the uncurling fronds of the lady fern, and catkins dancing high above in the cottonwoods. Salvator, as was her nature, shepherded Grace uphill, following behind, ears rotating backward and forward, nose swinging. She flicked her eyes up to check in with Grace before trotting off on her own. *Go*, Grace would say, setting the dog free to track down rabbits hiding in the blackberry thickets.

When they reached the top of the hill, the sun was warm above the fog. Grace lowered herself onto the loveseat, sometimes one side of it, sometimes the other. Because of the natural bend of the wood, one seat was higher than the other, and in her mind this was Samuel's seat, the other hers, although she liked to sit in both. Resting in his seat, she remembered his solemn eyes and tried to make her own eyes solemn as she thought about the serious matters in which he'd been involved: his belief in Peace, and in the Workers of the World. She herself had been a frivolous female, interested only in love. But Grace felt that begin to change as she sat there, just as she was sure it would have changed if she'd had more than one and a half years with him.

In late spring Salvator gave birth to a litter of three male puppies, her first, and a surprise, as Grace was unaware of any rendezvous with a sire. Still, it was wonderful to have the small, warm newcomers with their milky breath and blue eyes. As they grew, she found herself laughing at their rough-and-tumble antics in the house and around the yard. She did not notice anything peculiar about them, but the Pomo, when they returned to harvest the leaves of the yerba buena, commented immediately.

"They're half coyote," said Elsie, smiling the wide smile that showed off her small teeth, shortened from a lifetime of chewing willow and sedge for basket-weaving, Marie picked the puppies up one after another and sniffed their noses.

"My goodness," said Grace.

"Far-Seeing Woman says that you will have your hands full with these tricksters," said Marie (even though Far-Seeing Woman had not said anything).

Then Far-Seeing Woman did speak, softly, while her fingertips gently plucked the tips of the puppies' tails, so that each puppy turned to investigate its own wild wagging.

"What did she say?" asked Grace.

"She said that they will help show you the way. But it will not be in a straight line. It will be just like this. Turning in circles."

Grace did not know what that meant, but as she enjoyed the Pomos' visits and their advice, both practical and philosophical, she made tea for all of them and served it in her English bone china with the strawberry pattern. The women were greatly impressed with the design, turning their cups this way and that to admire them from all sides.

"The leaves of this plant are good medicine," said Elsie.

"For what?" asked Grace.

"For when you have the runny shits," said Elsie.

Grace burst into laughter.

"It's true," said Elsie. "In early summer, when the water in the river begins to drop and these fruits appear, you will find yourself in need of the medicine of the leaves."

During her second year in the cabin, when the wood of Samuel's memorial was weathering to a soft silver color, Grace began work on her second memorial. In a dream, she and

Salvator and her three half-grown pups, Hush, Groliere, and Tinman, swam through the river, the light sparkling off the tiny dimples on the surface where the blue dragonflies known as widow skimmers touched down. The salmon ran upstream around Grace's feet while a large brown bear stood amiably in the shallows on the opposite side, the river parting around it as it plunged its head under, waiting for a fish.

"So you have met the big bear," said Elsie, as Marie jostled her newborn baby on her knee.

"What does it mean?" asked Grace.

Far-Seeing Woman spoke at length, her old hands plucking at the air and tossing invisible things away, as if plant spores or blowflies were floating past.

"She says," said Marie, "that the grizzly bear is a visitor from the past. He has come to speak with you, who now lives on the land where he once fished."

"But what's he saying?" asked Grace.

"He is saying that you must remember him."

"I see," said Grace.

But only a few weeks later did she understand. Along the riverbank, as the dogs chased alligator lizards from under the rotting logs the winter floods had carried downstream, Grace sat on the beach, perfectly still, feeling a tingling in her skin. Flocks of chickadees alighted fearlessly in the salal bushes behind her and flung the piths of the berries around so it seemed as if it were raining dye. Grace's homemade flannel blouse was forever stained with this black splatter, and she wore the shirt throughout the making of her bear memorial.

In that moment of stillness she envisioned a fallen tree, a backrest against which a mother bear might lean to suckle her cubs, or a natural divan where an old boar grizzly could drape himself for an afternoon nap. There were many requirements for this tree in Grace's mind. It must have a pleasant view of the river, and it must inhabit that realm halfway between life and death, the trunk beginning to rot but with a few green needles still gracing its limbs. Grace knew she needed to think about the many elements of time, weather, the dogs, raccoons, and all the other erosive influences of her land in planning her memorial.

It should not be a real tree, she said to the dogs on their scouting trips to find just the right location, *because the point of it is human memory.*

Whenever Grace spoke aloud, Salvator paused in her rambles, turning her ears, if not her head, backward to listen. But the pups were beginning to reveal their wild nature. Their senses were attuned to a different language, which spoke to them from inside badger holes, from the bowls worn into dry trails where wild turkeys bathed in the dust, and from the wind, which carried snatches of bird dialect and coyote scent.

Grace began with chicken wire, as many bales of the stuff were lying around the old ranch, rusting in the open or smothering under rampant blackberry thickets. But after a single day of rescuing the rolls from near oblivion in leafy tangles, she found herself afflicted with a raging poison oak rash, which brought her work to a halt. She drove down to Ukiah for a bottle of calamine, and then later a second and a third, so that by the time the Pomo women came again she was caked in pink lotion, her skin swollen and weepy.

Elsie, in her practical way, set to work. She sent Marie out with instructions to bring back a large Oregon grape plant from the canyon east of the cabin where two creeks came together into a place the Pomo called Híwalhmu. Then she wandered along Grace's dirt road, bending gracefully from the waist and using a sharpened stick to dig out the bulbs of soap plants, which she set to roast in Grace's woodstove.

"You must eat one of these every day throughout the summer," she said, explaining how the plants grew together with the poison oak, their bulbs taking on a natural immunity that Grace would acquire by eating them.

Instructing Marie, Elsie oversaw the cooking of the grape plant and the rendering of its bark into a kind of lumpy glue.

"Take off all your clothes," she said to Grace.

Grace giggled. No one had seen her completely naked, not even her husband. The Pomo women teased her a little as she stripped, Far-Seeing Woman chuckling and pointing, their eyes widening at the sight of her pink nipples, the likes of which they'd never seen before.

Together, Elsie and Marie massaged Grace's body with the bark glue, using their fingernails to deposit it into the heart of the rash, slathering every square inch of her: the roots of her hair, between her toes, under her arms. The sensation of their scratching on her tormented skin was the most indescribably pleasurable thing Grace had ever felt, better even than the secret enjoyments she and Samuel had shared in the darkness of their bed together. Grace, who was self-conscious at first, soon began to ooh and ah, begging Marie to put a little more glue on that shoulder blade or behind that knee, until Far-Seeing Woman slapped her own legs and roared with laughter, shouting something in Pomo that made the other two splutter with glee.

"What?" said Grace.

"She says that if we're not careful, you will grow to love this so much you'll make sure to catch the rash every year."

· · ·

Grace worked on the bear memorial at a bend in the river near a water-cut bank of soil honeycombed with the tunnels of kingfisher nest holes. She placed her memorial above the stone-and-wood clutter of the flood line. The view was pleasant, a ridge of Douglas firs and redwoods, pebbled shores curving around shady pockets of water, and stands of black sage sweating their musky perfume. It was, Grace imagined, a place where a bear might be happy to rest while it perused the river.

She wrapped the sheets of chicken wire round and round each other to form a hollow cylinder about twelve feet long, then squeezed the diameter of one end narrower than the other, gathered the limbs of Douglas firs, and inserted them into the holes of the wire trunk. She mixed cement in a big tin washtub and slapped the thick concoction onto the chicken wire with a wooden spatula. Later she would mix a thinner, more pliable batch with which to sculpt the bark.

Far-Seeing Woman offered advice on the signatures left behind on bear trees, and Grace sculpted as best she could, using pieces of canvas covered with cement to simulate the strips of bark the animals bit and then pulled away from the trunks so they could lick the sweet, turpentiny pulp underneath. She etched the permanent record of their meal as teethmarks in the wood.

Grace visited this memorial often, leaning against it as the dogs dashed through the water chasing fish. The Pomo women were impressed with it, a fact Grace knew because on occasion she found offerings they left on the trunk: small bouquets of toyon berries or heaps of wild huckleberries nested in the orange petals of California poppies. But the greatest validation of her work came the first time she wandered down to the bear memorial and found a pile of coyote scat on the highest point of the upturned cement roots.

For the next few years Grace performed only the routine work of the seasons: chopping wood, burning overgrown grasslands (as Elsie advised her), and planting gardens. She spent most of this time alone except for the dogs, the occasional visits of the Pomo, and the even rarer summertime stopovers of friends from the city, whose calls became fewer and fewer as the years passed but who always arrived wearing high-heeled shoes, stockings, and white gloves, just the kinds of things that suffered badly from the dirt, dust, and brambles of Grace's world. The dogs wreaked havoc on the fashionable plumed hats her friends wore, stalking them with primordial patience, awaiting any opportunity to slink off and reassert their right to tear all feathered things to pieces.

For a while her old friends tried to matchmake, writing to her of this or that widower, or the tragic men who'd lost their fiancées, or the persistent bachelors waiting for the right woman. Grace paid them no heed. She had already married, and to her mind, death had not yet parted her from her husband.

Come, she'd say whenever these letters arrived, herding the dogs up the trail to the highest point on her land, the oak-covered ridge she called by its Pomo name, Kucádonoyo. She admired the dogs' stamina as they galloped backward and forward, up and down, three miles for every one of hers.

At the summit, on clear days she could see the ocean to the west, its surface bunched into long rows of swells, and to the east the snowy peaks of the Sierra Nevada, sitting like a mirage on an invisible blanket of air, or sometimes reflected upside down in the mirror of sky. On one spectacular spring day, so clear that for the first time she could actually see the foothills of the Sierra spreading softly and roundly, rootlike, into the earth, Grace came to see with some finality that she could never give this up, not for any widower, fiancé, or bachelor. In a few short years, given her inheritance and the unusual luxury of being a financially independent woman, she had arranged her life to her own liking, sharing decisions and responsibilities with no one.

Salvator raised a second litter of puppies, two females, who looked far more like coyotes than their half-brothers, with black-tipped tawny fur and orange eyes. Hoping to limit what might become an explosive dog population on her property, Grace had tried to keep Salvator inside when she came into season, and Salvator had suffered this indignity with stoicism, resignedly raising her eyebrows to Grace whenever Grace closed the door on her. But one night the temptation must have been more than the dog could bear, and Salvator burst through the window above the kitchen sink to make her escape.

Afterward Grace discovered the beauty in Salvator's sole act of defiance. Not only were the puppies canny, agile, with fine-tuned senses and remarkable courage, but they were clearly Salvator's pride and joy, the daughters with whom she would share her life. They learned and imitated Salvator's ways with startling rapidity, becoming (despite their coyote looks) more doglike than their half-brothers, staying close to Salvator and thereby to Grace. Grace called them Imogen and Cunningham, after the San Francisco photographer whose studies of plants and trees seemed to freeze time. This was how Grace felt

Salvator's daughters lived, moving unhurriedly, studying one durable instant of infinity after another.

That winter Grace was visited by Marie and Elsie, who traveled between storms on foot from their *rancheria* near Ukiah. When they arrived, their hair was soaked by the water still falling from the trees a day after the rain had stopped. Elsie stood by the woodstove to warm herself before removing something from the pocket of her patched coat and unwrapping it carefully from old newspaper.

"This is from Far-Seeing Woman," she said, handing Grace a small, exquisitely made basket.

The bottom half carried a star design woven in willow and redbud. The upper half was densely interwoven with soft pink feathers, so tightly stitched into the basket that they looked like fur. Grace turned it this way and that, admiring the details, including the arrow-shaped pieces of abalone shell hanging from the rim.

"It's beautiful," she said.

"Far-Seeing Woman had a powerful dream," said Elsie, "and in this basket she wove the story of her dream."

"The pink feathers are those of the mourning dove," said Marie. "The softest feathers from the breast and from under the wing."

"She had this dream many years ago," said Elsie, "before she met you, and yet it was about you. She knew this later."

Grace set the basket down on her little writing table so she could study it as she composed a note to Far-Seeing Woman.

"We will lay this down with her," said Elsie, reaching for the letter. Hearing her words, Grace pulled the envelope back.

"You don't know," said Elsie gently, "but Far-Seeing Woman was a Dreamer Woman. We will lay your letter down with her and she will read it from over there."

Grace sat suddenly down in her chair. Elsie and Marie brought her cups of tea and ran their hands down the back of her head, murmuring words in Pomo until she was willing to listen again.

"Far-Seeing Woman dreamed of many doves," said Elsie. "More doves than you could imagine. In her dream you were there, although she did not know you yet, but you were a child, and you knew something of one of these doves."

"What else did she say?"

"That's all. She said you would learn the rest."

For many months Grace wandered in her landscape, trying to understand what it was she would learn. She planted her vegetable garden in the spring and tended it throughout the summer, weeding the rows of squash and watermelon and to-matoes and peas as Salvator lay curled in the shade of the cornstalks, nose tucked into her tail, sleeping and dreaming. What did dogs dream of? Grace wondered. Of puppyhood and things long gone? Or did they dream even further back, to the days of their ancestors, the wolf-dogs, and before them the wolves?

One early autumn night Grace awoke, cold in the chill air before dawn, as she had not closed the windows the evening before. But that wasn't what had woken her. Latching the windows, she could hear the creek below, even months after the rains had stopped, its tiniest bells ringing softly as the water trickled over tree roots and rocks on its way to the sea.

In the spare bedroom where she kept a trunk filled with her childhood things she found her old scrapbook, and inside it a yellowed newspaper clipping that long ago, longer than she could remember, she had pasted there. It was the story of a passenger pigeon named Martha who had died in 1914 at the

Cincinnati Zoological Garden. Once, Grace read, there had been five billion passenger pigeons, almost 40 percent of the total bird population of North America. They had inhabited all the wild forests east of the Rockies and were considered to have been the most numerous bird species on earth. A Canadian naturalist in 1866 had watched a flock flying up from the United States that was at least three hundred miles long and one mile wide and that passed overhead in a solid mass for fourteen hours. But sportsmen shot them by the millions, and by 1914, Martha, age twenty-nine and alone in the zoo in Cincinnati, was the last of her kind.

Grace climbed back into bed in the first light of dawn, taking Far-Seeing Woman's feather bowl with her. The dogs, sleeping on bay-leaf pillows beside the bed, groaned and stretched and rearranged themselves in friendly piles of legs and noses and tails. Grace lay with the covers pulled up under her chin and turned the basket this way and that, thinking of the way doves and pigeons fly off with a characteristic clap of their wings behind their backs. Holding the soft feathered part of the basket up to her cheek, feeling the silky warmth, Grace imagined the evolution of such perfect form.

The details of her next memorial stymied Grace all through the autumn and a warm, wet winter that sucked storms up from the south and brought them ashore with enough rain to raise the river far higher than she'd ever seen it, high enough to spill into the woods and up the creek beds. The little cabin was in no danger, but the dirt road disappeared under a dangerous brown mass of downed trees and the lost wreckage from farm buildings upriver. Even when spring finally brought its winds to dry out the land and Elsie and Marie returned to collect the stems of the California hazel, even when Grace could at last tell them of her newfound discovery regarding Far-Seeing Woman's dream, she had not decided how best to memorialize it.

That spring as she rambled across her land, Grace studied the different ways of the dogs: Salvator, aging but always loyal, close to Grace's side; the male coydogs fanning out far off the trails; Imogen and Cunningham darting back and forth from Salvator to the news written on the ground in urine and scat. The dogs spoke to one another in their varied voices, barking, baying, and yodeling, and it was these sounds playing in the air that delivered the idea.

In her planning and execution, Grace made frequent trips to the blacksmith's shop just outside Ukiah, where she sketched her ideas for the old man with hands callused and scarred from a lifetime of burns. He did not, she believed, understand her vision, but he was hungry for work because of the Depression and eager to take on a paying project. He suggested that she use pig iron, poured from the blast furnace into pigs, or molds of sand. Grace drew him the templates for her design: equilateral triangles of various sizes, some no bigger than dinner plates, others as large as tires. She also requested that he cast seventeen clappers, round beads the size of baseballs, each with a hole through the center, as well as seventeen knockers about a foot long and in the rough shape of feathers.

At home she worked on the trestles, heavy, freestanding doorframes. She built them from madrone because of its hard wood, leaving the knobby elbows where the branches had been, sanding the red trunks smooth. Then she dug the post holes on a steep, grassy slope of live oaks that made up one flank of the mountain Kucádonoyo. With the help of the blacksmith's fifteen-year-old son, Hank, she erected the trestles, all seventeen of them scattered across the hill, facing east to west, awaiting the delivery of the chimes.

Hank helped again when the pig iron was ready, taking it upon himself to cut the Manila braidline with his knife and tie it into bow knots to hang from the heavy eyehooks on the underside of each trestle. Grace busied herself arranging the pairs of iron triangles on the ground and carrying them to the trestles. She and Hank worked together stringing the clappers and knockers onto the chimes so that when the wind blew, the feather-shaped knockers would swing the round clappers, which would then ricochet back and forth between the outer shells of the paired triangles.

As they worked, the pig iron clunked and clanged in baritones, basses, and tenors. But it would take a good wind to hear what they all sounded like in concert. A storm, Hank thought, his eyes lighting up.

In the end it didn't take a storm to give her memorial voice. The hillside she'd chosen was raked by winds funneled inland from the ocean and the chimes sang often, but differently during each season of the year. In springtime the seventeen chimes pealed nearly constantly on stiff winds. On summer days they rang suddenly in the afternoons, when the gusts heralding the coastal fog blew through, and then just as suddenly grew silent at the instant of sunset. They were quiet for long periods in the autumn, except when the diablo winds, the last hot breaths of Indian summer, tore in from the east, while in winter they became a kind of collective town crier, booming on the front edges of storms.

The first time Elsie and Marie and Marie's seven-year-old

daughter, Carmaline, came to visit the memorial, they brought baskets of food in memory of Far-Seeing Woman. Together with Grace and the pack of dogs, they set off up the flanks of Kucádonoyo for a late-summer picnic, complete with frybread made from the acorns of live oaks, the roasted and salted seeds of chia grass, a salad made with the fiddleheads of bracken ferns, apple-colored manzanita berries, and dried salmon jerky.

They wandered among the trestles, tapping the triangles to hear their sounds as Grace sat on the grassy hill below, watching them listen and think.

Grace continued to build. Through the war years, the boom years, war again and again, small revolutions on college campuses, scandals. Despite the proliferation of memorials, her property did not devolve into a junkyard of sculpture. Instead, her two thousand acres absorbed her work, revealing only glimpses: the flicker not of snakeskin but of a string of obsidian among the leaves of a box elder; the sound not of a frog but of a copper bell turning over in the creek.

With the passing of the dusky seaside sparrow, the ivory-billed woodpecker, the Bubal hartebeest, Grace grew older. The only mirror in her house was an ancient one, the silvering on its back thinned almost to glass, and so as the decades passed Grace's evidence of her own aging came mostly from her hands, the skin wrinkling and the fingernails thickening and yellowing. Seeing this, she began to investigate the dark territory ahead. Her work grew spare at first, then sharper, and finally subterranean: chambers dug into the earth, where the breath of life seemed suffocated. And yet Grace knew it was not. The coydogs could find it and grew mad on its scent, scrambling into the dirt, scratching at Grace's wooden cellars and stone basements.

Long before Grace came to this stage of her work, Salvator died, after a very long life for a dog of her breed. At the end she could no longer walk, and so each morning Grace carried her from her bay-leaf bed into the sunshine, a large black dog now shriveled to a fragile bundle of bones, as delicate and dark as a bat yet reveling in the warmth of the rays. Grace tended Salvator, the shepherd, and allowed the dog to die in her own time. It was the way Samuel had died, despite the brevity of his illness, with just enough time to prepare and to accept and finally, with grace, to go.

She buried Salvator on the slope of the hill beneath Samuel's bench and marked her grave with a small slab of granite hollowed in the center, where she nestled a golden crystal of cairngorm.

That night she dreamed a dream the likes of which she'd never had before. She was Salvator's puppy, unborn as yet, curled inside the dog's womb, and an amber light poured through the skin of Salvator's belly. Grace could feel her own dog nose, her pointed ears, the stub of a puppy tail. There within the womb she was dreaming a dream within a dream, a startling theater from another mind. Four feet galloping through grass, the world alive with the gritty poetry of scent, and sounds from registers she had never heard before: the crackle of trees growing, the snoring of waves on the coast miles away. But most remarkable was an instinct centered in her gut, a compass fueled by the beating of her heart, pointing her toward the center of her canine universe. Toward Salvator, the mother, and through her to Grace, the human Grace.

Innumerable dog generations later, a puppy was born who,

despite the preponderance of coyote blood and the occasional infusion of stray coonhound and pointer, seemed an exact replica of Salvator: by all appearances a purebred black German shepherd. He was named Goliath, a giant among the litter in both size and temperament. As Elsie had also died long before and Carmaline had moved north, only Marie, now an old woman like Grace, remembered Salvator and smiled in recognition as she picked up Goliath and sniffed his nose.

With Goliath and the pack dancing alongside her, Grace started a new stage of work. She began to explore entirely new materials, ones that would not perhaps last as long as iron, cement, and stone but in the course of their delicate existence might offer clarity.

High in the trees or down among the dry summer grasses, Grace places empty window frames. Through these, she imagines, visitors might someday glance in order to see not through the glass but through the glassless frames to transparent elements on the other side. To a sliver-thin mobile of mica, a handblown glass pipkin, a gossamer curtain. As Grace builds, old words from the *OED* pour forth, and the sound of her voice in solo conclamation delights the dogs, who wag their tails and woof, not knowing or caring that these words hark from lost and nearly forgotten languages.